WE WISH YOU A HAPPILY EVER AFTER

ELENA AITKEN

We Wish You A Happily Ever After

Copyright © 2020 by Elena Aitken

ISBN: 978-1-989685-25-9

Chapter One

"10-4. I'M ON MY WAY." Jeremy Davis shook his head and muttered a silent curse as he ended the radio call, flipped his lights and sirens on, and as safely as he could on the icy mountain roads, steered the fire truck into a giant U-turn in the middle of the highway to head in the opposite direction.

Next to him, his new partner, rookie Natalie didn't even bother hiding the broad smile that crossed her face, and Jeremy had to work hard not to laugh. It wasn't that long ago that he was an overexcited newbie, eager for every call.

He pressed down on the accelerator as soon as it was safe to do so. His heart raced, the familiar adrenaline flowing through his veins the way it always did when there was an emergency fire call, which admittedly, and thankfully, wasn't very often in the quiet mountain town of Glacier Falls.

Which was why Jeremy had been using his afternoon to head out to the Ever After Ranch with the ladder truck to help out the Turner sisters with their latest big idea for a Christmas open house. The entire town was excited for the event, and even if Jeremy wasn't secretly a huge fan of all things Christmas, he would have volunteered his time to help the ladies out with the lights.

But not today.

At least not yet.

Not when there was an actual fire call to respond to.

"What do you think it is this time?"

Jeremy simply sighed in response, because it was a fair question. They were on their way to Roy Burton's house for the second time that week—and the fourth time that month. Beyond the fact that the old man was increasingly becoming a danger to himself, he was also starting to be a danger to those around him if the limited resources of the Glacier Falls fire department were regularly being called to his house to put out his forgetful fires. As the second-in-command at the department, the chief had asked Jeremy to *handle* the situation, which meant that it would be Jeremy's job to report Mr. Burton's state to the appropriate authorities if he believed it to be a real problem. Roy was a longtime resident of Glacier Falls, and a beloved neighbor, but he didn't have any family in town, and that made things a little trickier. Especially because, as far as Jeremy knew, his family hadn't visited him in years.

The fact was, the old man shouldn't be on his own. It was only a matter of time before something really serious happened. And because Jeremy had grown up in Glacier Falls, where Roy Burton was largely regarded as the town grandfather—to the point where he even played Santa Claus every Christmas—Jeremy was fond of the man. Almost as if he were his own family. "Could be anything," he said after a moment, hoping upon hope that it was once again a minor issue. He wouldn't be able to live with himself if something happened to Roy because he'd failed to act sooner.

He stepped on the gas pedal a little harder.

It only took another few moments to arrive in front of the familiar bungalow in the middle of town. Lydia Arthur, Roy's neighbor, stood on the sidewalk, wearing a puffy, full-length parka over her dressing gown. With her feet jammed in clunky boots and a long wool scarf wrapped around her head, her arms waving frantically as the truck pulled up, she looked every bit the concerned neighbor, the way she did every time they arrived.

There was no obvious signs of a fire inside the home—a fact Jeremy was grateful for—but it also didn't mean anything. They moved quickly: Jeremy ran to the front door, while Natalie went to Mrs. Arthur to see what she could learn, which very likely was a variation on the story they heard every time.

"I called and he didn't answer."

"I knocked on his door and he didn't answer."

"I smelled something unusual."

Some might think that Lydia was simply a nosy old woman, but Jeremy knew better. Her interest in Mr. Burton was more than simple neighborly interest. The older woman was definitely sweet on Roy. Anyone could see it.

"Mr. Burton?" Jeremy banged his fist on the wooden door and, without waiting for an answer, tried the handle. Unlocked. "Roy?" he called out as he entered the home. "Are you in here?"

Before he could take more than a few steps in the door, Jeremy was hit with the acrid smell of burnt food. He quickstepped it into the kitchen, spotted the flames inside the oven, and quickly flicked the dial on the controls to turn the heat off. The safest thing to do was to let the fire burn itself out inside the oven. Opening the door would only provide oxygen to fan the flames.

"Roy?" Jeremy turned away from the oven to scan the rest of the kitchen. The man was nowhere to be found. Which meant he was probably napping. One last look toward the oven, where the flames were almost out, and Jeremy assessed the situation safe enough to go in search of the man, whom he found in the living room, fast asleep on the couch. His hearing aids were on the table next to him.

Gently, so as not to startle him, Jeremy sat next to Roy and shook his shoulder until his eyelids fluttered open. "Roy. It's Jeremy Davis." He spoke in an excessively raised voice as he gestured to the table with the hearing aids. "I'm sorry to wake you, but I—"

"What is going on in here?"

A female voice behind him caused Jeremy to turn. The woman was silhouetted in the doorway with the low afternoon sun behind her. Jeremy couldn't make out her face, but something about her was familiar. He moved to stand and greet the woman, but before he could, she dropped the bag she was holding to the ground and pushed past him.

"What is wrong with my grandfather?"

Grandfather?

Seeing Papa laying on the couch, the giant fireman towering over him, stopped Bella's heart for a moment. The groceries that had been so important that she couldn't wait until later to pick them up were forgotten as she dropped them to the ground and rushed to his side past the firefighter, who, from what she could tell, was only in the way and if anything, confusing her grandpa.

"Papa? Are you okay? What happened? Why do I smell smoke? Were you—"

"Bella?"

The firefighter said her name, which only annoyed her because she knew who *she* was. What she didn't know was what had happened.

"Bella Hoffman?"

She spun around to look at the idiot man who wasn't doing

4

anything to help her. "I go by Burton actually. Is there someone in charge here?" she demanded as she looked past the imbecile in front of her, out the door where she'd seen another firefighter, a woman, speaking to Mrs. Arthur when she'd returned to the house. "Where is the other one?"

"The other…firefighter?"

"Yes." She was quickly losing patience. "I need someone who is in charge to tell me what happened and what is wrong with my grandfather. When I left him, he was doing just fine and going to have a—" As her own words filled the room, she realized what she was saying. She turned back to her grandfather, who was now struggling to sit up and put his hearing aids in at the same time.

"A nap?" The annoying firefighter finished for her with a smugness to his voice that made her see red. "Were you having a nap, Roy?" He leaned in next to Bella, and the fresh, crisp scent of him filled her, causing her to momentarily forget that she was completely unimpressed by his presence.

She shook her head and refocused on the real issue. "Papa? Are you—"

"Having a nap," he interrupted her with a chuckle. "At least I was." Papa looked between her and the firefighter, whose nearness was starting to distract her on a cellular level that was increasingly frustrating. "What's happening here?"

"Yes." Bella spun to the other man, a move she instantly regretted because he was standing much closer than she thought. She came practically nose to nose with him but instead of bumping into him, she took a step back and hit her leg on the coffee table that had trapped her between the couch and the firefighter, who seemed to have grown in size in the last few seconds.

He grabbed her shoulder, preventing her from crashing hard on her bottom, and held her a moment longer than was necessary.

"Are you okay?"

She nodded, momentarily unable to speak, which was ridiculous because she was never at a loss for words, especially if it involved a man. And never in an emergency situation, which she had to assume they were still in.

"We had a call that there was a fire," he said, still holding her shoulder.

She nodded as if it made sense, which it didn't. The fact that there was a fire truck outside and a firefighter standing in front of her notwithstanding.

"A fire?"

"In the oven."

"In the—oh shit." Her hand flew to her mouth as she realized exactly what had happened.

The frozen lasagna she'd popped in to heat up before running out to the store to get the garlic bread and salad so she could serve Papa a *home-cooked* meal. Or at least, a *home-prepared* meal.

The man in front of her chuckled. "I assume you had something to do with that?" He looked strangely relieved, even though there was nothing about the situation that called for relief.

She nodded and shook her head all at once.

Beside her, her grandfather had risen to his feet, a smile on his always friendly face. "You thought it was me again, didn't you, Jeremy? Joke's on you this time. I told you I'd be more careful."

It took Bella a moment, but she stared at her grandfather. "What do you mean, *again?* Does this happen a lot? And..." She turned to the firefighter, who all of a sudden she was looking at in a new light. "Wait. Jeremy?"

There was no way.

"Jeremy Davis? Who I used to play hide-and-seek with when I came to visit?"

His handsome—and much more grown up than she remembered—face split into a smile. "More like hide-and-forget." He nodded. "It's good to see you, Bella. It's been… what…ten years?"

"Thirteen."

His eyes went round and he shook his head. "Wow. That long, hey?"

"My Bella here isn't much for the mountains," Papa said.

Even though she knew it hurt her grandfather that she hadn't been to visit him, there was still so much pride and love in his voice. It only made her feel guiltier.

"Besides, you can't become a famous singer in the middle of nowhere," he continued. "The city has always been where she belongs."

The twinge of guilt in her gut sharpened into a full-out pain.

"A singer, huh?" Jeremy gave her an appreciative look. "Your voice always was amazing. Good for you."

"You remember?"

He grinned, his lips twitching up at the corner. "I remember a lot of things."

Despite herself, a blush heated her chest, threatening to creep up her neck.

"If you two are done flapping your gums, can you leave me to my nap?" Papa broke the awkwardness, which a moment later only got more awkward when he added, "Bella, is that lasagna done yet?"

Jeremy lifted an eyebrow as his lips widened to a full-fledged grin. "Lasagna, huh? You might need different dinner plans."

Bella took a deep breath and let it out slowly. "How about we chat in the kitchen?"

The last thing she needed was her grandfather thinking she wasn't able to take care of things. Especially considering she'd been in town less than twenty-four hours and she was here to help *him* out over the holidays.

The moment she was in the kitchen and out of earshot, she spun around and slammed directly into a very hard chest. She'd expected him to follow her, but not that close. And she definitely hadn't expected that kind of brick wall chest.

Then again, what did she have to base it on? A fourteen-year-old version of Jeremy Davis? Probably not a great comparison.

Bella took a step back and for the first time looked at her old friend properly.

His shoulders were massive—must be the jacket.

He was ridiculously tall—must be the boots.

And his chest—well, she already knew that felt like something chiseled out of stone.

No, he was definitely not the skinny, slightly goofy teenage boy she remembered.

Before she could say anything, Jeremy spoke. "Burton?"

She shrugged. "I decided to go with my mother's maiden name. It has a nicer ring to it for my career."

"Makes sense." He nodded. "So, Bella *Burton*, it was you who started this fire?"

"What do you mean, *this* fire? Also, what actual fir—" The question died on her lips as her eyes landed on the blacked-out window of the oven door. "Oh."

She turned back to Jeremy, who was nodding.

"I assume you had the oven too high or—"

"Shit."

He cocked his head.

"I forgot to take the cardboard off the top." Bella realized how it sounded as she said it. It couldn't sound any other way. But still, she'd been in a hurry and that's exactly what had happened. "I was distracted," she said by way of explanation. "I was trying to…never mind." She didn't need to explain to this relative stranger that she'd been trying to impress her grandfather and do something nice for him, but was already running late when she showed up and in her haste had made a ridiculous mistake.

Her shoulders fell as she looked again at the oven. *Maybe she'd just order takeout?*

"Don't worry about it." Jeremy put a hand on her arm and instantly, her body reacted the way it had earlier when he'd stopped her from falling. "But I do think we should talk about all the other calls we've had to Roy's place lately and—"

"Jer?"

An impossibly young woman dressed in matching fire gear appeared in the doorway.

"We gotta go."

Jeremy nodded in her direction. "Busy day. But we should talk later, okay? Are you in town for a bit?"

Bella nodded.

"Great." Jeremy squeezed her arm one more time before he turned and left the room.

She heard him say good-bye to her grandfather before he left. Then the door closed with a thunk, and Bella was left feeling lonely and oddly excited all at the same time.

Chapter Two

BELLA.

Bella Hoff—Burton. He mentally corrected himself. It did have a nice ring to it.

Bella Burton.

What were the odds?

Jeremy shoveled another load of snow from the drive of the firehall and tossed it over his shoulder. It had been snowing for the last two days straight, which wasn't unexpected for December in the mountain town of Glacier Falls, not at all. But it never failed to take some residents, and particularly some of the tourists, off guard and cause some very busy days as Jeremy and the rest of the crew responded to a never-ending list of fender benders and cars in a ditch.

Fortunately, none of the incidents he'd responded to had been very serious and staying busy wasn't so bad.

Unless you had other things you wanted to do.

Like talk to Bella Burton again.

And he very much wanted to do that.

And not just about her grandfather, although discussing Roy Burton's memory loss was also at the top of his list. Particularly because Ed Walker, the fire chief, had asked him more than once about Roy's status. Ed and Roy were old friends, which was part of the reason Ed wanted to take a bit more of a hands-off approach—he didn't want his feelings about Roy to compromise the decision—and also because Jeremy was certain he was trying to give him more responsibilities. Perhaps in preparation to taking over as chief one day. Either way, Jeremy wasn't the only one who was concerned about the old man's wellbeing.

Obviously, if Bella was in town, Roy's family must also have concerns. Not that they'd been to visit him in…well, probably since the last time he'd seen Bella.

Bella.

Jeremy shook his head with a low whistle.

Who would have thought she'd grow up to be so friggin' gorgeous?

He would have.

At least, when he was in his late teens, he used to daydream about how she'd turned out. And he'd had some damn good guesses. She'd been sixteen the last time he'd seen her. He'd been fourteen. Barely more than a child. But old enough to experience his very first, very strong, crush on a girl and experience his first kiss.

And his second.

For almost three years, when he was a kid, he'd been obsessed with Bella Burton. Old enough to notice that Bella was…*Bella.*

When he was a kid, her parents would drive her out to Glacier Falls and drop her off as quickly as they could before jetting back to the city to spend a summer child-free while Bella ran wild in the woods with her grandfather, and whatever kids her age were available to play. Which, for at least a few years, included Jeremy.

His summers with her were some of his fondest memories, and not just because of the kisses on that last hot August night before she'd gone home for school. In the time before the internet and texting, they'd exchanged a few phone calls, and only one or two letters—turned out, Jeremy wasn't much of a pen pal—but it had fizzled out and when she hadn't come to visit the next summer, he'd gradually forgotten about her.

Mostly. Not entirely.

She'd always been at the back of his mind.

An unanswered question.

And now…here she was.

Finally, after thirteen years he could—what?

What could he do?

Jeremy couldn't help but laugh at himself because obviously his fantasies had gotten the better of him. They'd been kids last time they'd seen each other, playing kids' games.

A first kiss at fourteen was a whole lot different than—well, everything else. And just because his imagination had spun elaborate stories of what could have been didn't mean that was reality.

No.

The reality was that Bella Burton may be back in town, but they were virtual strangers to each other. A few shared summers when they were kids meant nothing. Not really. And worse, there was the whole matter of her grandfather, Roy. He couldn't imagine Bella would be very happy to hear that they were on the verge of calling social services in. Everyone was worried about the man's welfare, and it wouldn't be long before they were pushing to have the old man moved into a nursing home facility, where he would no longer be a danger to himself.

Jeremy couldn't imagine that Bella would be happy to hear that. No granddaughter would.

Which was why he needed to be the one to talk to her. It would be easier to hear coming from a *friend*. Old or otherwise.

He shoveled the last load of snow onto the now towering pile and turned around to examine his work. With the snow still coming down in large, fluffy flakes, the drive was already covered in a thin layer. No doubt, he'd be out there clearing it again a few more times before the day was done. Jeremy made a mental note to look into the department's budget to see about a snowblower.

Ed Walker always said it was an unnecessary expense, but maybe if Jeremy was going to be in charge soon, he could finally make a case for it. He straightened his shoulders, excited the way he always was, at the prospect of being appointed fire chief. Even in a small town like Glacier Falls, it was a big deal and a much bigger job than he probably realized yet. But Jeremy was up to the task and more than ready. He'd worked hard, and he loved his hometown. He'd happily serve as chief, taking the good with the bad.

First things first. Jeremy tucked the shovel inside the garage and shook the snow from his parka.

He needed to go find Bella.

"It's beginning to look a lot like—ow!"

The box Bella was pulling off the shelf shifted and slammed into her shoulder. She jostled and only barely stopped herself from falling off the step stool as she regained her balance.

"What was that, Bella? Are you okay?"

"I'm fine, Papa. Just getting the Christmas decorations down like you asked."

When Bella agreed to the task, she hadn't realized the boxes were kept on the very top shelf of the storage room and were heavier than…well, pretty much anything she'd ever lifted, ever. After dragging the second box down and lugging it up the basement stairs into the living room, Bella was completely out of breath. She dropped into the easy chair next to her grandfather, who'd already started digging through the first box she'd brought up.

"Were you singing down there, baby girl?"

Without opening her eyes, she nodded in response.

"I thought so. It was beautiful."

Bella opened one eye then and looked at him. But he wasn't looking at her. Instead, he gazed at the snow globe he held in his hands. She knew the one. Inside the glass was a tiny house with two carolers standing in front of it. Bella knew if you wound it up, it would play "Silver Bells," her grandfather's favorite Christmas song.

"Remember when you used to sing to me, Bella?"

She nodded, but when he still didn't look away from the globe, she spoke. "I do. Every Christmas when you came to visit, I'd sing you all the carols in front of the tree."

It was a fond memory. The only time Bella's parents could convince him to come and visit them in the city was during the holidays. Otherwise, they had to go to him, or as was more often the case as Bella got older, only she would visit, her parents too busy working in the city to take any time off. Or, more likely, not wanting to use up any vacation time on a trip to the mountains, when it could be used for a sunny beach down south instead.

"And in the summer, I'd sing them all to you again," she added and he laughed.

"Just a silly old man wanting to hear Christmas songs in the heat of the summer."

He turned to her and she couldn't help but notice the shine in his eyes. *Had she ever seen Papa cry?*

"But your voice was like an angel, and they were the only songs that we both knew all the words to."

Bella pushed up from the easy chair and sat next to him on the couch. She carefully lifted the snow globe from his hands and cranked the toggle until the sweet melody of *"Silver Bells"* played and she began to sing.

The sound of singing stopped Jeremy from knocking on the door.

He listened to the beautiful voice. It had been years since he'd heard it, but he'd know it anywhere. Only now, Bella's voice was deeper. Richer and silkier somehow.

A woman's voice.

She always did have a talent for singing, and it was no wonder she'd been able to make a career out of it. After Roy had mentioned it, he couldn't stop himself from doing a quick search on social media. Sure, he probably could have just asked her what she'd been up to since they were kids, but he couldn't seem to stop himself.

Not wanting to disturb the singing—and selfishly, wanting to hear it better—Jeremy very lightly knocked on the door and let himself in. Roy saw him from across the room and smiled before turning his full attention back to his granddaughter, who was lost in song.

He didn't dare move, lest she see him and stop, so he stood as quietly as he could, his eyes glued to Bella. Her thick, dark, curly hair was pulled back into a ponytail, with strands escaping around her face. She wore a knit sweater over her jeans and even with the simple outfit, she looked glamourous.

She'd always spoken about being a professional singer one day, and from the posts and announcements Jeremy had scrolled through, it was clear she'd made her dreams come true. She was the lead singer in a jazz group, Velvet Heart. Jeremy tried not to judge it by its name, but they seemed pretty successful and Bella had even posted on her Facebook that she'd be recording an album soon.

He could see why.

Anyone who could take a simple Christmas carol and make it sound the way Bella did was pure talent.

A moment later, the song was over and, unable to help himself, he started to applaud.

Bella spun around and stared at him, her mouth open. But a moment later, she laughed. "Do you always just let yourself into my grandfather's house?"

"Seems I do."

"Come in, Jeremy," Roy ordered. "Don't just stand there lurking. Maybe Bella will sing you a song, too? What's your favorite Christmas carol?"

Jeremy shed his jacket and boots, and walked into the room. "Do you only sing Christmas songs?"

She shrugged. "What's your favorite?"

"Mine is 'The Christmas Song,'" he answered without hesitation.

"A little chestnuts roasting on an open fire, hey?"

"What's yours?"

"If I tell you, will you sing it with me?" She tilted her head and before he could answer, she said, "'Baby, It's Cold Outside.'"

"That's a duet."

She laughed. "Which is why I asked if you'd sing with me."

He reached up and scratched at the scruff on his chin as he shook his head. "I don't think that's a very good idea."

She smiled and a shot of desire raced through his body. *Did she have any idea how sexy she was when she smiled?*

"How about a cup of hot chocolate then?" Bella stood. "I'll make us all one. With extra marshmallows," she added with a squeeze to Roy's shoulder.

Both men watched her as she left the room.

"She's something else, my Bella." Roy shook his head with wonder. "I've sure missed her. But I guess that's the price you pay when you move out to the mountains. Your family is far away, and they never come to visit."

There was a longing in the old man's voice as he spoke. It had never occurred to Jeremy that Roy might be lonely, but of course he would be. Even when you were surrounded by good friends and neighbors, there was something different about the love of a family. It was clear that Roy loved his granddaughter deeply.

"Well, she's here now," Jeremy said. "How nice that she came for the holidays."

Roy's face lit up. "Such a nice surprise. She called and said, 'Papa. I'm coming to visit.' And the next day, here she was."

"That is a nice surprise." *For both of us.*

"She's going to be a star, that girl."

Jeremy chuckled at the man's certainty. "I don't doubt that for a minute." There was a crash from the kitchen, and Jeremy jumped up. "I better go make sure she's not lighting your oven on fire again." He laughed, but when Roy looked confused, he instantly regretted the joke. After all, there was a chance that Roy didn't remember the events of the other day, or at least not all of them. His laughter died on his lips. "I'll go give Bella a hand."

"I'm really not usually this clumsy in the kitchen," Bella said for at least the third time since Jeremy had found her on her hands and knees, cleaning the broken mug that had slipped and shattered on the tile when the boiling water splashed onto her hand. "I swear, I can't remember the last time I...well, to be honest, I actually can't remember the last time I cooked a meal."

She laughed when Jeremy raised an eyebrow at her.

"Just being honest."

He shook his head with a chuckle that made his eyes crinkle in the corners. He dumped the rest of the broken pieces into the trash and wiped the spill before taking a new mug from the cupboard. She watched as he easily measured out hot cocoa and poured equal amounts of water into the mugs.

"You know your way around."

"In general? Or in Roy's kitchen?"

She shrugged. "Both."

"I do a lot of cooking at the station." He winked at her. "Not that making hot chocolate can be counted as cooking."

It was absolutely crazy, but when Jeremy looked at her that way, her stomach fluttered wildly. Crazy because it hadn't done that since she was sixteen. And even more crazy because she barely knew him. Not really.

"And my grandfather? You really do seem pretty comfortable here." She'd been thinking about it ever since the other day when she'd lit the oven on fire. It wasn't the first time Jeremy had been there. "You said something that gave me the impression that my little oven fire wasn't the first time you'd been called out."

Jeremy's face changed. The easygoing lightness was replaced by a frown that darkened his features. "I actually wanted to talk to you about that."

The butterflies in Bella's stomach died abruptly, turning into heavy stones. Jeremy wiped his hands on a towel and tossed it over his shoulder in a casual way that Bella would have, under any other circumstance, found incredibly sexy.

"About what?" she heard herself ask and immediately felt stupid. She knew exactly what Jeremy wanted to talk to her about. She'd noticed it herself in the few days she'd been there. But somehow knowing something bad was different than knowing you were going to hear it from someone else. It seemed worse somehow. More real.

Jeremy gestured to a chair at the table but she shook her head. It would be easier to get it over with.

He nodded in understanding and pressed his lips together. Despite herself, and the heavy conversation she knew they were about to have, dirty images involving herself and those lips flashed through her mind. She shook her head in an effort to clear it. If he'd noticed her lapse in concentration, he didn't mention it.

"We're worried about Roy," Jeremy said without any preamble. "The other day was the second time this week that I've answered a call."

"To be fair…"

He smiled a little. "It was your fault," he finished for her. "I get that. But it doesn't take away the fact that the number of concerning episodes is increasing. We think maybe it's time to consider moving your grandfather into a—"

"Don't say it."

"Bella." Jeremy reached out and squeezed her forearm the way he'd done the other day, and her body reacted the same way it had then, in a full-body vibration. *What was it about this man?*

She took a step back, not wanting it, but *needing* the space between them. "What do you mean *we*?"

He looked confused for a moment.

"You said that *we are concerned*," she explained. "Who is we?"

Jeremy nodded and once again pressed his lips together. "Natalie and I."

A girlfriend.

Shit.

A wife.

Of course Jeremy would be taken. He was gorgeous and a firefighter, and he obviously had a heart of gold if he was so concerned about her grandfather. Why wouldn't he be snapped up?

But why did it matter? Especially right now.

Still. The thought of some other woman. Some *Natalie* having discussions about Papa with Jeremy upset her in a completely unreasonable way. She scrubbed her hands over her face and tried to smooth her ponytail. A pointless task with her wild curls. She straightened her shoulders, and did the only thing she knew how to do in the situation. She got defensive.

Jeremy knew the conversation would be hard. After all, how many grandchildren who adored their grandparent wanted to hear that they were becoming a danger to themselves?

But, for a moment, he thought it might actually go easier than he'd assumed. Bella had even seemed to be on the same page with him, maybe already thinking what he was. That would have made things easier.

But then something shifted.

"Look." Bella's voice was icy in a way he'd never heard before. "I don't know what you and *Natalie* think. But you don't know my grandfather. And if the two of you don't have anything better to do than talk about Papa while you're sitting around in the evenings sipping wine or whatever it is the two of you do, then I don't know how to help you."

Wine?

Evenings?

What was she talking about? Jeremy didn't sit around drinking with his partners. Even when they were off shift, Natalie never—*oh.*

He couldn't stop the smile from stretching across his face when he realized the misunderstanding and exactly what it meant.

Bella was jealous.

"What's so funny?" She put her hands on her slim hips in a move that was so completely adorable and totally ridiculous at the same time. "Jeremy!"

He forced the smile off his face and looked down at his feet. "Sorry. I don't mean to—"

"Laugh at my grandfather's situation?" She stomped a foot and again, Jeremy had to bite back a laugh. "It's not funny."

He cleared his throat and looked up. The moment his eyes met hers, the laughter died. She might be jealous in a seriously sexy way, but more importantly, she was filled with concern for her grandfather. She was terrified.

"Bella." There was no trace of humor as he stepped forward and took her in his arms. To his surprise, she let him hold her. "I'm sorry. It's not funny. Not even a little bit. Roy is becoming increasingly forgetful, I'm sure you've noticed."

She nodded against his shoulder and he stepped back. Her deep-green eyes shone with unshed tears, but they didn't spill. She sniffed hard and nodded again.

"I've noticed. It's hard not to."

He nodded knowingly. "And that's why Natalie—my rookie partner," he added quickly before she could react again, "and I are worried. The chief is asking me to recommend to social services that maybe it's time he's moved to a nursing home or a facility where he won't be a danger to himself but still have a high quality of life." Her pretty face was a mixture of emotions and questions. "Part of my job is to work closely with other community agencies, like social services. In this instance, since you're in town now, I wanted to come to you first before getting social services involved."

She nodded and he watched as her face relaxed again. She'd definitely been jealous. An interesting observation he'd examine in depth later. Now wasn't the time.

"You're right," she said after a moment. "It's hard not to

notice and my mom, even though she never actually visits, talks to him a few times a week on the phone and she's mentioned his memory loss as well. I'm going to talk to the doctor, too, but…" She sighed deeply. "We all agree that it might be time to get rid of the house and move him."

"I know it's hard."

She dropped her head for a moment before looking up quickly. "I'll bring it up with him and I'll do my best to get him to agree, but I'm not forcing anything until after Christmas."

Jeremy wasn't expecting that. "I assumed you would—"

"Christmas," she said with more authority. "No move until after Christmas. You didn't see the way he lit up when he started going through his old decorations. I can't do that to him. He needs one more Christmas in his house. He loves it."

Jeremy didn't know Roy well, but he did know that much about the man. After all, he was the town Santa.

"Okay." He found himself agreeing. He'd deal with the chief. "And you'll stay?" He couldn't be sure whether he was asking for Roy or himself. "Until after Christmas?"

She looked him in the eye and nodded slowly.

He turned quickly so she wouldn't see the grin that he couldn't stop, and grabbed two mugs of the cooling hot cocoa. "We should get these out to Roy."

Chapter Three

"THIS IS THE LAST STRAND." Logan Langdon handed Jeremy another bundle of lights and Jeremy couldn't help but raise an eyebrow in question. Logan had been telling him "just a few more" for over an hour. Jeremy's fingers were numb from cold, and even in his thick parka, he was starting to shiver.

"I promise," Logan said in response to his unanswered question.

"It is." Levi Langdon, Logan's cousin, chimed in. "You're lucky Hope is on bed rest, or she'd demand lights on *all* the trees."

From his perch on the ladder, Jeremy looked around the Ever After Ranch that was surrounded by dense forest and laughed. "I don't doubt that for a minute. How is Hope doing, anyway?"

Levi's face lit up. He and his wife, Hope—one half of the Turner twins—were expecting their first child in a few months. It was a bit of a tricky pregnancy due to an earlier cancer diagnosis, but despite some bed rest as a precaution, everything seemed to be going just fine. "She's doing really well, but with

Christmas coming and some weddings booked up, she has these grand plans to create a winter wonderland out here."

"Right," Logan chimed in. "Which means we're basically at her beck and call creating it." He complained, but he wore a wide grin on his face. Logan had recently married Faith, Hope's twin sister, and was just as head over heels in love with her as Levi was with his wife. Jeremy had no doubt that both men would do whatever they could for the women they loved and the wedding business they were all part of.

Ever After Ranch had been solely run by Hope, but Faith returned to town the previous spring to take over when Hope got sick. Right around the same time, Levi had returned to Glacier Falls and it didn't take long for him and Hope to remember how much they'd loved each other when they were kids. So when they decided to get married and go traveling before starting a family, that left Faith alone to run the business. Thankfully, Logan stepped up to help Faith out. It was clear to everyone else in town that he'd been in love with Faith since… forever. And sure enough, it only took a few months for them both to realize it once and for all.

Not that Jeremy begrudged any of them their happiness. They were all great people—his best friends, really—and they all deserved to be happy. But he'd be the first to admit that sometimes it wore on him that everyone around him seemed to be finding their happily ever after while he…*what?*

Jeremy shook off the mood that threatened to descend over him and climbed up to the top of the ladder one last time to string up the last of the lights.

Twenty minutes later, they were warming up in the house with mugs of steaming coffee thawing their hands.

"I really appreciate it, Jeremy." Faith set a plate of baked goods in front of him and reflexively he looked to Logan, who laughed.

"They're from Sweetie Pies," Logan said with a laugh,

earning him a smack to the arm. "Stephanie keeps us stocked in baking. I swear I've gained at least ten pounds."

Stephanie was the twin's half-sister, a pretty recent discovery that had changed the dynamics of the Turner family. "You think *you've* gained weight," Stephanie said as she walked into the kitchen. She rubbed her flat stomach and groaned. "But I can't seem to stop myself. It's just so good and after being on every no carb, low carb, no sugar, no dairy, no wheat diet out there for as long as I could remember, well…" She shrugged.

"It's a good thing you don't have a role to prep for or anything," Faith said. "Or maybe it isn't good. Seriously, we could all use a little less baking around here."

"No roles coming up?" Jeremy had never known a celebrity before, and Stephanie Starz was the very definition of celebrity. In fact, she'd recently been named one of the *hottest* movie stars in the world.

"Not yet." Stephanie grabbed a scone and sat at the table. "I'm taking time off but still looking at a few scripts. If something really awesome comes up…" She tore off a piece of the baked good. "But I've been thinking I might want to do something else, too. Maybe a…never mind. It's dumb."

"It's not dumb," Levi said. "It's a great idea." He turned to Jeremy. "She's talking about opening a little retreat center."

"Not so much a center," Steph interrupted. "Maybe just some cabins." She shrugged. "I don't know. It's still very much in the idea stage. I was talking to Nick about—"

"Nick, huh?" Faith wiggled her eyebrow. "How is Nick?"

Jeremy had to laugh at the family. They reminded him of the soap operas his mom used to watch when he was a kid, only with less angst. Mostly the family seemed to get along pretty well, but it wasn't unusual for at least one of them to have some kind of drama going on.

"Nothing is going on between Nick and me." She spoke

with such authority that no one questioned her. "We're only friends. I haven't even really spoken to him since he left town with the baby."

The baby.

It was hard to forget that particular dramatic turn of events. In September, at Faith and Logan's wedding celebration, a stranger had shown up out of the blue with a baby, claiming it was Nick's responsibility. He'd been pretty much MIA since then, dealing with the details of exactly what it meant to have a baby thrust into his life.

Jeremy still didn't know the details about what had happened; as far as he knew, nobody did. Nick had been in the city pretty much since then, and if anyone knew what was going on, they weren't saying.

And he didn't ask. Soon the conversation shifted to Christmas, and the festivities they were planning, including the orphan dinner on Christmas Eve that the fire department put on every year.

"You'll all be there?" he asked unnecessarily.

"You know we will." Faith smiled. "I'm looking forward to it. I haven't been in years. Is your family going to be there?"

Jeremy shook his head. "Not this year. Mom and Dad went to visit my sister, Charlotte. She's been living on the East Coast. So I'm on my own."

But maybe not. The conversation swirled around him, but Jeremy was only half listening as he let his thoughts drift to the one person he'd really like to be celebrating the holidays with. Ever since Bella had mentioned she'd be staying for Christmas, he couldn't help himself from making a bit of a Christmas wish for himself.

One he certainly hoped would come true.

Bella put the brochures for the assisted living homes on the kitchen table in front of her grandfather and pasted the biggest smile she could on her face.

"This one looks nice, don't you think?" She tapped a finger at the glossy picture of a home in the city, close to her parents' condo downtown. "It has a pool."

"A pool?" Papa looked at her as if she were the one who'd lost her mind. "Do you think I care about a pool?"

"You might." She knew she was grasping at straws. "It could be a lot of fun to take one of those classes with the music and belts where you kind of run in the water."

Her grandfather eyed her suspiciously. "You think that sounds fun?"

She couldn't help it. Bella laughed. "No," she admitted. "It doesn't."

She dropped her head in her hands and massaged her temple. She'd convinced her parents to let her talk to Papa about moving. She thought he might take the news better from her, but so far, despite her best attempts, he was not buying into the idea.

"Bella. This is my home. I don't want to move to the city."

"But, Papa. You can't stay here." She looked up. "It's not safe. Jeremy said the fire department practically has your house on autopilot."

"Fine."

Bella looked up cautiously. There was no way she'd just spent over thirty minutes trying to convince her grandfather to move and now, just like that, he'd agreed. She knew better. Bella narrowed her eyes and tilted her head. "What do you mean, fine?"

"Fine. I'll move." He took a sip of his tea. "But not to the city."

Ah.

She knew it was too easy.

"But, Papa, that's where we all live."

"No." He put his mug down. "That's where *you* all live. I live here. And I will not have my family's poor life choices affect my life."

She couldn't help but laugh. "The mountains are gorgeous."

"Damn straight they are." He looked at her seriously. "But that's not why I stay." He waved his hand to dismiss her over-simplification. "The mountains put everything in perspective. Strip away the noise of the city and the busyness so you can find yourself and everything that's really important. The city has a way of muting you."

Bella thought about that. Had the city muted her? She didn't know the answer because the city was all she knew. It's all she'd ever had.

Not true.

She'd had the mountains once before, too. When she was young. Some of her favorite summers had been spent in Glacier Falls. It felt like a million years ago that she'd felt the freedom of her youth. It was almost a wildness that had flowed through her.

She'd never stopped to think of it before, but it was only when she'd stopped visiting her grandfather that it had changed. But Bella had been too busy working on her career. Taking every singing gig she could get, paying her dues, performing all night in smoky dive bars, falling into toxic relationships, trading the neon lights of the downtown strip and a *muted* version of herself for the wild child she'd once been.

But that was the only way to make it.

Bella would have laughed at herself if it hadn't been so deeply sad—because she *hadn't* made it.

As if Papa knew exactly what she was thinking about, he chose that moment to ask the question she'd been avoiding. "When is your album coming out, Bella?"

"You're changing the subject." She grinned and shook her head.

"No." He was firm. "I said I'd move. Just not to the city."

He raised his eyebrow and Bella had to shake her head with a small sigh. *Baby steps.*

"Now answer the question. When's the album coming out?"

Bella forced a smile on her face. "Soon." It was a lie. The truth was there would be no album, not after discovering Kyle —her sort-of boyfriend, the leader of Velvet Heart, the band she was in, and the man who had creative control over the album in question—in bed with another woman. Kyle hadn't thought it was a big deal, but Bella had a different opinion. One that she expressed in the form of yelling and throwing all of Kyle's things—including his guitar—out the window of his studio apartment to the street below.

Her little tantrum, followed by her subsequent quitting of the band and leaving them in the lurch right before a gig had pretty much guaranteed she was out of the record deal. Never mind the fact that she no longer had a band to play with, or well…much of a career left at all.

All details she didn't think needed to be shared with her grandfather at that moment. After all, it's not as if it would change anything if he was disappointed in her.

"I'm working on a few things, Papa." She forced a smile to her face. "But I think the most important thing to work on is getting this house ready for the holidays, don't you think?"

He watched her carefully, but finally gave her a nod. Papa wasn't a stupid man. Even if his memory was starting to fail him, he wasn't going to fall for her lies that easily, and she knew it. With any luck, she could distract him long enough to sort something out.

Papa pushed his chair back from the table and stood. "I

agree." He dusted his hands together. "Jeremy should be here any moment."

At the mere mention of his name, her heart fluttered and a blush came over her before she could stop it. "Jeremy? What does he have to do with anything?"

Chapter Four

"I NOTICED a tree lot down by the hardware store when I came through town the other day."

Jeremy didn't even try to hide the shock on his face when he turned to Bella, who sat next to him in the cab of his truck. Close, but still too far away for his liking. He silently cursed his oversized truck. He'd prefer to have her closer. *Much* closer.

"A tree lot?"

Bella blinked hard. "Where else would we get a tree?"

He couldn't help it; Jeremy burst out laughing. "I'm not sure if you've looked around lately, city girl, but we're surrounded by trees. Almost all of which would make the perfect Christmas tree."

When Roy had called him at the station to ask him a favor, Jeremy had jumped at the opportunity. If it involved spending the afternoon with Bella, he was in. Hell, if it involved spending *any* time with Bella, he'd make it a priority. And he was pretty sure Roy knew that. The old man was smarter than most people gave him credit for, but Jeremy saw right through him. He had ulterior motives, for sure. Not that Jeremy was complaining. He took another look at Bella in her red puffy jacket, her dark hair spilling out under a knit cap. She looked so perfectly at home in Glacier Falls.

She belonged there.

Except she didn't.

He needed to remember that. Glacier Falls wasn't her home. And she'd be leaving again.

But that didn't mean he couldn't enjoy his time with her while she was there.

And that's exactly what he planned to do.

"So you mean…"

"We're going to go into the woods and cut down a tree." Jeremy grinned. "But not just any tree." He winked at her and had to resist the urge to put his hand on her leg. It was incredible, and a little scary, how comfortable he felt with her so quickly. "We're going to find *the* tree."

"You're serious?" She laughed and it was such a full sound in the cab of his truck that Jeremy instantly wanted her to do it again. "We're going to cut it down?" She turned so she faced him. "Like with our bare hands?"

"Well, I don't know what your hands are made of." He laughed along with her. "But I thought maybe we could use an ax."

She smacked him playfully.

"Does that sound good?"

Bella nodded before turning back to look out the window of the truck, where it had started snowing. "It sounds amazing. I can't believe we never came to Glacier Falls for Christmas. Papa always came to us. Until he started playing Santa, that is. Then he'd only come if it didn't interfere with his duties."

Roy had made a great Santa. He himself had fond memories of more than one Christmas Eve where he'd sit on his lap and, with wide eyes, tell Santa all the things he wished for. And most of the time, those wishes would come true.

He glanced over at Bella and couldn't help but wonder

whether that strategy would work now. If he told Santa what he wanted for Christmas, maybe she would stay and—

"I ran into Katie at the store the other day."

The name of his ex-girlfriend coming from the lips of the woman he was currently contemplating making Christmas wishes about startled Jeremy into reality.

"Did you?" He tried to sound casual. "I didn't think you even really knew Katie."

"Of course." She laughed. "I mean, I didn't think I'd actually recognize her, but her voice was a dead giveaway. She still has that same bubbly personality, doesn't she?"

Jeremy nodded. He didn't know how much Bella knew about his relationship with Katie. Not that it had ever been much of a relationship. Mostly just an on-again/off-again thing through high school and…well, beyond. Not that he'd actually thought it would go anywhere. Which it clearly didn't, because she'd recently married her best friend, and his high school buddy, Damon Banks.

He'd be lying if he said it hadn't taken him off guard, though. Truthfully, Damon and Katie were the best match and it had just been Jeremy's pride that had been wounded. He really was happy for the two of them, even if their coupling forced him to face the fact that he was alone.

"She's married now," Jeremy said. "To Damon. Remember him?"

"Of course!" She spun again in her seat and her eyes gleamed. "Even when we were kids, he was tall and oh, those eyes."

Despite himself, Jeremy felt a flash of jealousy in his gut. *Bella had noticed* Damon's *eyes?* But it had been him she'd spent all her time with. It had been him who she'd—

"I always knew they were into each other. The way they looked at each other." Bella laughed. "I don't think they even knew what was going on, but…you can't miss a connection like that, even when you're too young to know what it really means."

"Do you really think that?"

He caught her gaze and held it for a moment before turning back to the road. He'd happily look at her all day if he wasn't trying to navigate a snowy logging road in four-wheel drive.

Did they have that connection?

He was no expert, but dammed if he didn't think they did.

He *knew* they did.

"So you're enjoying your time back in town?" He was digging, but he couldn't help it. Maybe if she liked it here, she'd stay and then…

"I am." She grinned. "There's something absolutely magical about being in the mountains in the winter. I had no idea. It's like living in a snow globe." She laughed again, and the sound filled him.

"It's like that all the time." Jeremy slowed the truck and pulled it into a snowy clearing. "A pretty awesome place to call home, actually." Before she could respond, he put the truck into park and killed the engine. "Ready to go find the perfect tree for your snow globe Christmas?"

———

Snow slid down between her leggings and the boots Bella wore, soaking her socks and chilling her toes as she followed Jeremy through the deep snow, but she didn't care. They'd warm up, but she'd never get this moment back.

Your snow globe Christmas, he'd called it. She couldn't have described it better if she'd tried. That's exactly what it was like, being in Glacier Falls for the season. Absolutely magical.

And spending time with Jeremy was just an added bonus.

Something about being with him was just—easy. It had always been that way.

Bella stopped walking for a moment and tipped her head back. The fat, wet snowflakes falling from the sky blanketed her face. Feeling like a little kid, she held her arms out and spun around as a giggle rose from deep in her throat.

She couldn't help it; she spun faster and faster until finally she fell into the pillowy snow, her arms and legs outstretched. In the perfect position, she started to wave her limbs and make a snow angel.

"Having fun?"

She opened her eyes to see Jeremy standing over her, a gorgeous smile lighting up his face.

"So much fun."

He didn't wait for an invitation, a fact she secretly loved, but instead flopped down next to her and started to make his own snow angel.

"See? So fun."

"It is fun."

Bella turned her head to see Jeremy propped up on his elbow watching her.

"You're going to wreck your angel," she protested. "You have to get up slowly so you don't—" Her words died on her lips. "What?"

"You have snowflakes on your eyelashes." He reached out and for a second she thought he might try touching her lash. But instead, he held out his hand and in a swift move, hopped to his feet.

Bella accepted his hand and a moment later, Jeremy pulled her easily up from the snow and her angel and into his arms.

His mouth was only inches from hers. His arms wrapped around her and he held her close. "You look gorgeous covered in snow."

And then his lips were on hers. He tasted of peppermint

and cinnamon, and his kiss melted her. Literally. The snowflakes on her lashes turned to water dripping down her cheek.

Bella laughed and pulled away to wipe at her face, but when she was finished and her eyes once more locked with Jeremy's, she found something besides laughter there, and it made her stomach twist into knots.

She should turn away. She should pick out her perfect Christmas tree and get it home to Papa.

But then again…what was the rush?

Before she could overthink it, Bella reached out and put her mittened hands on either side of his face before pressing her lips to his in a deeper kiss than before.

Vaguely, she registered a low moan. *Was it her?*

It didn't matter.

She had no idea how long the kiss lasted, but as far as she was concerned, it wasn't long enough before a gust of wind slapped their cheeks with fresh, arctic air.

"Oh, that's cold." A chill ran through her and she shivered.

Jeremy looked up, but didn't take his hands off her arms, a small fact Bella appreciated. She liked his touch. Maybe more than she should. That kiss, and then the one after that, had sparked something inside her that had been dead for years.

Thirteen, to be exact.

"Could be a storm blowing in." Jeremy rubbed her arms a little. "You think you'll be warm enough for a few more minutes?"

There were a million flirty ways she could have answered that question, but they all eluded her at that moment. In fact, all words escaped her. She nodded in response.

"Okay." If Jeremy noticed her sudden case of muteness, he didn't say anything. "Let's go get that tree. There are some good ones over there." He started to walk in the direction he'd pointed to.

It took Bella a moment, but she soon followed after. She needed to remember why she was there. *To get a tree. To have a memorable Christmas with Papa. To help him move into a new place.*

And then she needed to get back to the city and pick up the pieces of whatever was left of her career.

She was *not* there for a relationship.

Who said anything about a relationship?

Bella watched Jeremy's back, a few steps ahead of her, and a smile crossed her face.

Who was *saying anything about a relationship?*

No one.

"How about this one?" Jeremy called out.

She brushed off the idea before it could completely take root and hurried over to where Jeremy stood next to a tree.

Chapter Five

"IT'S PERFECT!" Bella hung a glass ball on the branches of the tree she'd personally chosen and cut down with only a little bit of assistance from Jeremy, and stood back to admire her work.

"It is perfect," Jeremy agreed. "As were the other dozen we found before you settled on this one."

He smiled and shook his head, because he'd had no idea she was such a perfectionist. Especially when it came to Christmas trees. They must have looked at twenty of them. Their toes and fingers were numb before she'd finally chosen one.

"You picked a beautiful one, Bella." Roy wrapped an arm around her and squeezed. "Thank you both for getting it. I can't remember the last time I had a tree of my own."

Bella turned and stared open-mouthed at her grandfather. "What? But you love Christmas."

"It doesn't mean I always got my own," he answered matter-of-factly as he picked an ornament off the table, where Bella had laid them out. "It didn't make a lot of sense to have a tree just for me."

Jeremy didn't miss the shadow that crossed Bella's face at her grandfather's admission.

"Well, I'm glad you have one now," she said. "These ornaments are far too beautiful to be tucked away any longer." She picked up a ceramic angel and admired it before placing it on the tree. "Are you going to help?" she asked Jeremy as she caught him leaning against the wall watching them.

He shook his head. "I was actually going to excuse myself." Decorating a tree was a family affair. He'd had a lot of fun getting the tree, but he had no place in Roy's living room with him and his granddaughter.

"What?"

"Nonsense."

Roy and Bella both spoke at the same time and he laughed. "No, really. I should get going. You two enjoy yourselves."

For a moment, it looked as if Bella would protest, but he really wished she wouldn't. As much as he enjoyed spending time with her—and he did—he had his limits, and he was about to reach them.

Being around her without pulling her up tight against him so he could feel every inch of her through that thick sweater she was wearing was getting harder and harder. He needed to take his leave before he did anything X-rated in front of Roy.

"I'll walk you out."

He said his good-byes to Roy, promised to come back soon to admire the finished tree, and walked out the door to the porch. Bella pulled the door shut behind her and, without missing a beat, he pulled her into his arms and kissed her hard.

"I've wanted to do that ever since we—" He shook his head. "Ever since we finished the last kiss."

She bit her bottom lip, sucking it into her mouth a little, and he groaned.

He was definitely doing the right thing by leaving now while he still had a little self-control.

"Damn, Bella. I—"

She silenced him by pressing a finger to his lips. "Will I see you soon?"

He nodded.

Damn straight she would.

"Good." She winked and, without another word, disappeared back into the warmth of the house.

Despite the wind that had definitely picked up and heralded a coming storm, Jeremy stood there for another few moments, not really feeling the cold before slowly exhaling.

When it came to Bella, he was in so much trouble.

He knew it. And he didn't care a bit.

As much as she hadn't wanted Jeremy to leave, Bella had to admit, it had been a good decision. Spending the time with her grandfather as they hung each ornament was special. She'd never before spent a holiday with him at his house, so she'd never seen any of the ornaments they carefully hung on the tree. Even more special was the way Papa told her about each one, where it came from and the meaning behind it.

And they all had a story.

Bella loved it.

"What about this one?" She held up a delicate glass snowflake. "It's beautiful."

Papa's face transformed, a sad smile taking over. "That was the first ornament I bought your grandmother," he said. "The first Christmas we were married. We didn't have much money, but I wanted to give her something beautiful. Worthy of her and my love for her."

"It's gorgeous." Bella swallowed past the lump in her throat. "I bet she loved it."

He nodded slowly. "She sure did. She always hung it in the

middle of the tree, so you could always see it." He squeezed his eyes shut for a moment. "Will you hang it, Bella?"

"Of course." She carefully stepped over the boxes and paper strewn on the floor, and carefully threaded the ribbon of the ornament onto a branch, making sure it was nestled securely into the branches before stepping back to admire it.

"It's perfect. Your grandmother would approve."

Bella turned to look at Papa. "I wish I could remember her." The emotion she'd been trying to swallow down threatened to bubble up. She wasn't usually a crier, but then again, it wasn't every day she shared such a special moment with her grandfather.

Papa reached out for her hand, and she gave it. Bella let him guide her to the couch, where they sat, her hand still in his. "You are so much like her," he said. "You look like her."

Bella nodded. Her grandmother had died when she was a baby but she'd seen pictures, and she did look just like her. From her wavy, dark hair to her green eyes, she was almost a carbon copy of her except for the fact that Bella had a few inches on her grandmother's five-foot frame.

"And your voice." Her grandfather shook his head. "You sing just like her. Like an angel sent from heaven. She would be so proud of you, Bella."

She doubted that. There wasn't much to be proud of. She'd spent most of her adult life living in cheap apartments, taking whatever gig she could get and hoping for her big break. And she'd thought she'd had it, too, if it hadn't been for Kyle. Or maybe it was her temper that had gotten the best of her? Maybe she shouldn't have cared that he was sleeping with other people. After all, they weren't exclusive. Still...

Bella shook her head. "I don't know, Papa. I haven't done anything much to be very proud of."

He shook her hands and forced her to look at him. "Are you kidding me, Bella? You are living your dream every day and working hard to see it realized. These things don't happen overnight, baby girl. They take time and the only way to achieve your goal is to try. That's what you're doing. Every day. Your grandmother would be very proud of you. Just like I am."

A tear slipped from her eye and she let it fall to her lap. His belief in her was so strong. Maybe it was enough for both of them.

"Do you know why I moved to Glacier Falls all those years ago?"

She shook her head. Her mom said something about how he'd wanted to run away after her grandmother died, but Bella always thought there was more to it than that.

"It was always your grandmother's dream to live in the mountains. Did you know that?"

Bella shook her head.

"We talked about it and planned how we'd do it one day. But something always came up to stop us. There was always a reason not to do it. So we'd put it off for later. But then she died and there was no later." He took a breath. "So I did it. Just the way we should have when she was alive. I took the leap, quit my job in the city and got on at the hardware store here in Glacier Falls. Your mother never could understand why I'd trade that life for this one, but your mother never had a dream like mine." He squeezed her hands together again. "Like yours."

They sat in silence for a few minutes while Bella absorbed everything he'd said.

"Thank you, Papa," she said after a while. "I needed that. I think maybe I've lost faith in myself for a bit."

He laughed and released her hands. "Nonsense. You've always had it. You've just forgotten for a moment." He pushed up from the couch and selected another ornament to hang.

"And one more thing..." He handed her a felted snowman. "Keep your eyes open."

"What?"

He chuckled. "There's always more than one path to get where you're going, and if you aren't paying attention, you could miss the path that will change everything."

She wanted to ask him what exactly he meant by that, but he didn't seem interested in talking anymore and she didn't want to push him.

"You know what would be good? Some hot chocolate. There's nothing like hot chocolate when you're decorating the tree."

Bella laughed and kissed him on the cheek on her way into the kitchen.

Unwilling to go home to a quiet apartment, Jeremy instead headed to the Knot, the local pub. It was Thursday, guys night. Or what had been guys night. To be fair, he hadn't been to the Knot on a Thursday in months, so he couldn't be certain it was still a thing. For a while, he'd avoided going because Damon was back in town and married to Katie. It had gotten a little awkward after Jeremy had punched him that one time, but then he'd just gotten busier and busier with work. And truthfully, when he did have a quiet night, he was more inclined to spend it relaxing in front of the TV before he fell asleep.

Probably not the best thing for his social life, but he was pretty sure the guys wouldn't hold it against him.

Sure enough, there were a few familiar faces around the usual table at the back of the room. Logan, Brody, and Damon greeted him with smiles and fist bumps when he grabbed a stool and pulled it up to the table.

"Good to see you," Damon said. "Really. It's been a long time."

Jeremy nodded. They'd been close once. Hopefully they

could put all the Katie stuff behind them, and get back to that. Especially because, for Jeremy, it really was already behind him.

The men slipped into easy conversation, catching one another up on what was going on in their lives and with their wives. Jeremy still thought it was crazy that they were all married. It was a strange thing to see your childhood friends grow up and turn into responsible adults. Strange in a good way. Although, at times, Jeremy caught himself wondering whether he'd ever meet a woman he'd want to marry.

At least, he *had* wondered that.

A smile crossed his face as an image of Bella filled his mind. He shook his head and lifted his beer to his mouth, but not before Brody noticed.

"What's that smile all about, Davis?"

"It's nothing." He tried to redirect the conversation to the subject at hand—Nick Newton and the baby who had shown up in a strange woman's arms the night of Logan and Faith's wedding. Jeremy didn't know Nick very well. He was a new friend of Damon's from the city. A billionaire due to the microchip that they'd developed and sold, making them wealthy beyond their wildest imaginations. Nick had come to Glacier Falls for Damon's wedding and never left. Jeremy himself hadn't had much of a chance to get to know him, although he seemed like a nice enough guy. And then the baby had shown up and Nick left. "I was just thinking that while I feel for Nick being blindsided that way, I'm glad it wasn't me."

All the men nodded in agreement, but Logan narrowed his eyes in question. "For sure," he said with a nod. "But I don't—"

"Has anyone heard from him?" Jeremy cut his friend off before he had a chance to dig any deeper. "Stephanie said she hadn't, but they were close, weren't they?"

Logan shook his head. "I don't know about close, but they

were getting to know each other, I guess. And from what I understand, she hasn't heard from him. Damon?"

Damon shrugged and lifted his glass. "Only a few short texts to say he's figuring things out. Knowing Nick, we'll get answers when he's ready. Until then…"

"Until then, maybe Jeremy can tell us about Bella."

Jeremy almost spat out his beer. He wiped his mouth and turned to Logan, who sat back with his arms crossed over his chest and a smug look on his face.

He looked around the table for help.

Brody, who was pretty new to town himself, shook his head and chuckled. "Who's Bella, Jer?"

Damon raised an eyebrow and grinned.

Jeremy muttered a curse word under his breath and spoke to Brody, because the others knew damn well who Bella was. "Bella is an old friend," he explained. "She used to spend her summers here with her grandfather when she was a kid."

"And Jeremy was madly in love with her."

He shot Logan a look. "I was a kid."

"Doesn't mean you didn't love her." He shrugged. "I know a bit about that."

Jeremy couldn't help but laugh because Logan had been in love with his now-wife, Faith, since they were kids. Even though he hadn't outright admitted it, they all knew it was true.

"And now she's back?" Brody prompted. "To stay?"

"No. Which is why, even if there was something—which there's not," he added quickly. A lie and they all knew it. "Nothing would come of it. She's a professional singer. Glacier Falls is no place for her."

"Tell that to Steph," Logan said. "She's quite literally the most famous actress in the world right now and she's not in a hurry to leave. She's talking about buying land."

"I don't think Bella is in the market for any land in the middle of nowhere." Jeremy looked down into his almost empty beer glass and for a second allowed himself to think about what that might look like. *Bella staying in town.* It looked good.

Very good.

"She's only in town for the holidays." Saying it out loud left a sour taste in his mouth.

"You should bring her to the ranch on Saturday."

Jeremy looked at Logan. "The ranch? What's on Saturday?"

"Don't tell me you forgot. No, wait, tell me you forgot," he added with a grin. "Because Faith will kill me if she thinks I forgot to invite you. I didn't, did I?"

Jeremy laughed at his friend as his memory came back to him. "I didn't forget," he said but added, "Okay, well, I did. But I remember now. That's why you needed *all* the lights."

"Exactly." Logan raised his glass. "Bring Bella. It will be fun. We'll have sleigh rides and hot chocolate and a big bonfire in the yard. Very festive."

Jeremy nodded. *Cuddled up in a sleigh with Bella?* It did sound like fun. A lot of fun.

Chapter Six

BELLA HADN'T BELIEVED Jeremy when he told her that they could have warm days in the mountains. Especially considering it had taken her two full days to warm up after their tree-cutting expedition. But he was right, and it was a perfect winter day. The sun shone in the blue sky, making it almost warm enough to unzip her jacket. *Almost.*

She'd been excited to join Jeremy at Ever After Ranch for a day of Christmas festivities and not just because she wanted to spend more time with Jeremy—although that definitely factored. Ever since arriving in Glacier Falls, she'd been excited about Christmas in a way that she hadn't been since she was a little girl. Spending the holiday with Papa had a lot to do with it, she was sure. He genuinely enjoyed every single moment of the season. The day before, they'd spent time in the kitchen trying—and mostly failing—to recreate some of her mother's Christmas baking. All recipes that apparently used to be her mother's. But if her grandmother and her mother had the baking gene, Bella certainly hadn't inherited it. Which was why she'd ended up in town at Sweetie Pies, buying a platter of Christmas baking.

Either way, they'd had fun trying to make them work. And as far as Bella was concerned, that's what it was all about. She'd enjoyed making memories with her grandfather more than even she'd expected to. It made her sad to think that she'd missed out on so many other holidays in Glacier Falls. Why her parents had insisted on Christmas in the city was beyond her, because there really was something magical about spending the season in the mountains.

Bella wasn't completely unaware. It wasn't just spending time with Papa that was helping her have such a good time. She glanced over at Jeremy, who caught her smiling at him.

"What's that for?"

"Nothing." She winked at him. "I was just thinking about how much I've been enjoying my time in Glacier Falls."

"Oh yeah? Spending time with your grandfather?"

It was cute that he was fishing for her response, but Bella couldn't help but let him dangle on the line a little longer. "It really has been great," she answered honestly. "I had a small breakthrough with him the other day. He agreed to move."

"He did?" Jeremy genuinely looked surprised.

"Well, he agreed to move out of his house. But he refuses to move to the city."

"That seems reasonable."

Bella turned to face him. "It does?"

"Glacier Falls is his home. There's some great seniors homes here in town. Why would you want him to move to the city?"

She hesitated. "Because that's where we live."

Bella didn't miss it when he flinched. *What did that mean?* Before she could let herself dwell on the possibility, she quickly looked out the window right as they drove through the gates of Ever After Ranch. "At any rate, it's a start."

"It is," he agreed. "I'm sure you'll find him a great spot

where he'll be happy, and safe. And…you know if you need a hand with anything, I'd be happy to help."

"Thank you." She glanced over at him again as he parked his truck next to a line of others in the Ever After Ranch yard.

Spending so much time with Jeremy had definitely helped her get in the holiday spirit. It had also helped her feel things she wasn't sure she'd ever felt before.

"You ready for this?" He smiled and reached across the cab of the truck to squeeze her hand. "There's going to be a lot of people."

"Great," she answered honestly. "I love people." Bella couldn't help but laugh. "And it's been a long time since I've seen most of these guys. I'm really looking forward to it." It was an honest answer. "Thank you for bringing me."

Bella held Jeremy's gaze for a moment before he leaned across the space and pressed his lips to hers. "I assure you, it is very much my pleasure."

A shock went through her all the way down to her toes that were cozy in her warm boots.

There'd never been another man who'd given her that type of thrill from a simple kiss. In fact, she'd forgotten that feeling existed at all. She'd been sixteen the last time she'd felt it. When she'd kissed Jeremy for the first time.

Bella would have happily stayed in the truck kissing him all day, but before she could even attempt to sway him to her way of thinking, he'd hopped out of the truck and had opened her door.

"Ready for some festive fun?" Jeremy offered her a hand that she took.

"Absolutely."

The moment her feet hit the ground, she heard the music mixed with the jingling of bells and she had to laugh.

"What's so funny?" Jeremy wrapped an arm around her

waist and pulled her close. It was such an intimate move, but it felt perfectly right.

"It's just so…" Bella shrugged. "Christmasy. I kind of love it."

"It's pretty awesome, isn't it?" Jeremy led her toward the barn, where the horse-drawn sleigh had just pulled up. "And this is my favorite Christmas carol."

"It is?" Bella tilted her head to hear it better. "It is," she said, remembering that he'd told her a few days earlier. "The Christmas Song." Jeremy nodded and she started singing. "Jack Frost nipping at your nose."

Jeremy's smile encouraged her, so she kept singing.

When the song was done, he pulled her in for a quick kiss. "And now it's really my favorite."

"Sorry, I couldn't help myself. It's just so festive."

"Don't apologize. It was amazing." He squeezed her hand and used his free arm to gesture to the trees. "As soon as the sun goes down and the lights come on, I think you'll be even more impressed. The girls did a great job. Oh!" Jeremy pointed toward a small group. "Speak of the devils. There they are. Come on. I want to introduce you."

Bella laughed. "I've met them before, remember?"

"Doesn't count," he said as they got closer. "We were kids then."

She stopped short, forcing him to stop as well. "We met when we were kids, too."

Jeremy turned and wrapped her up tight in his arms. "It's not the same. We're…" Instead of finishing his thought, he kissed her thoroughly, right in front of everyone by the barn. A fact she only remembered when a few whoops and hollers of appreciation sounded.

"Don't just stand there kissing her all day." A beautiful blonde woman, who Bella instantly recognized as one of the Turner twins—which one, she never could be sure—squeezed between them, breaking up the kiss. The woman turned to chastise Jeremy with a waggle of her finger before looping Bella's arm in hers and tugging her toward the waiting crowd.

Fortunately, Bella didn't embarrass easily because for the next few minutes she was fawned over and teased about spending all her time with Jeremy.

They were all so welcoming that, just as when she was a kid, Bella felt right at home. It didn't take long before she was laughing and joking with everyone as if they were old friends. Which, in a way, they were. The blonde turned out to be Faith. But her sister, Hope—who was pregnant and on bed rest—joined them as well from a wheelchair that she clearly hated.

"It's a means to an end," she told Bella as she rested her hands on her blanketed stomach. "If it means that this little one is safe and sound, then I'll keep sitting and let everyone wait on me hand and foot." She laughed and reached up to take her husband's hand.

"You know I'll go to the ends of the earth for the two of you, babe." Levi bent down and kissed her on the forehead. It was such a sweet and touching moment, that Bella felt as though she were intruding.

"They do that all the time." Stephanie Starz, the movie star, joined her and shook her head with a laugh. "They *all* do it." She rolled her eyes but Bella could see that she didn't really mind. "It's hard being the only single one around this group." She groaned but then laughed. "But hey, it's better than being stuck with someone you shouldn't be, am I right?"

Bella had never considered herself the type of person to get star struck, but she found herself at a loss for words with the bubbly, beautiful redhead who she'd only ever seen on the big screen or on magazine covers up until that point. The fact that she'd turned out to be Faith and Hope's older half-sister, who'd been adopted as a child, was still big news everywhere.

"You're not the only single person, Steph." Jeremy had

joined them again. He put his arm around her again as if it were the most natural thing in the world, and they'd been a couple for years, or were even a couple at all.

"Oh yeah, right." Stephanie shook her head. "Like you're single." She raised an eyebrow and laughed.

She stiffened a little and laughed along with her new friend. *They weren't a couple.*

She glanced over at Jeremy, who wasn't laughing, but was watching her with a question in his eyes.

Or were they?

"Sleigh bells ring! Are you listening?"

Even though they were all singing along to the carol, Bella's voice rang out clearer than the others as the horses pulled the sleigh through the snow. Jeremy was transfixed by Bella's voice.

Hell, Jeremy was transfixed by Bella.

It felt so right to be with her. He'd been a little worried that it would feel strange to be around all his friends with her considering they weren't really a couple, but it hadn't. Not even a little bit. In fact, it had felt absolutely perfect. He didn't want to think about what those feelings meant. Or what it might mean when the holidays were over and Bella went back to the city. She'd laughed when Steph suggested they were a couple. But that didn't really mean anything.

It was something they hadn't discussed yet. *And why would they? They'd only been—*

"Your voice is amazing!"

Jeremy's train of thought was interrupted by Stephanie. She'd moved herself to the hay bale across from them and had grabbed Bella's hand, effectively jerking her forward and out of his arms.

He missed the feel of her next to him, but he couldn't help but laugh at Stephanie's gushing.

"Are you professionally trained? You sound like an—"

"Angel," Jeremy couldn't resist finishing for her. "She does." He winked at Bella, who grinned.

"Thank you," she said to both of them. "I sing in a…well, I…" Her smile twisted into a quick frown before she glanced over at Jeremy and quickly caught herself. "I sing professionally, actually."

"Well, you're amazing. Do you have any originals? Or even better, an album I could listen to?"

"Steph, leave the poor girl alone," Logan called across the sleigh. "We have time for one more carol before we get back to the ranch."

"How about '*We Wish you a Merry Christmas*'?" someone yelled. A moment later, the whole group was caught up in the tune, and Bella was once again tucked into the crook of his arms.

It had been a perfect day, as far as he was concerned. The sky was blue and while the sun was out, it had been warm enough for sweaters, especially when they skated on the little rink that had been set up. Now that the sun had gone down, it had cooled off considerably, but Jeremy wasn't upset about that at all because it meant he could pull up the fleece blanket over their laps and pull Bella even closer to keep warm.

Under the cover, when her hand slipped to his leg and squeezed his thigh, a jolt of desire shot through him. It was all he could do to keep from pulling her up onto his lap so he could kiss her the way he'd been dying to all day, right then and there.

He could wait.

As it turned out, Jeremy had to wait even longer than he'd expected to because when the sleigh ride wrapped up, Levi had a bonfire going in the yard, and they were shuffled along with the rest of them to warm up with a cup of cider next to the fire. It was late by the time they walked through the ranch yard, under the twinkling lights he'd helped to hang, and back into the truck.

"That was a fun day." Bella sank back against the seat. "But I'm exhausted."

He tried to hide his disappointment, but obviously wasn't successful at his efforts, judging by Bella's chuckle.

"If you're tired, I'll take you home, but—"

"But I'd rather go back to your place."

He turned so quickly in his seat, she laughed again. Harder this time.

"Is that okay?"

For a split second—but only a split second—Jeremy thought about playing it cool. And then his instincts kicked in and he closed the distance between them and did what he'd been wanting to do all day: kissed her hard and without question as to what his answer was.

Chapter Seven

JEREMY'S APARTMENT was a third-floor walkup that backed onto the river just off Main Street. It was tastefully, if not simply, decorated and clean. Those were the only details that Bella registered as he unlocked his front door and stepped inside to turn the lights on. He'd barely had a chance to turn around when she was in his arms, kissing him.

Bella had never been shy when it came to men and getting exactly what she wanted. She'd never had trouble feeling sexually empowered and had no problems initiating as long as it meant she'd get what she wanted. Something about Jeremy felt different, though. With him, she'd been a bit shier than she'd ever been. Maybe it was because they'd known each other when they were kids. She'd been his first kiss. Not hers, though. Billy Johnson had been her first kiss in fourth grade. By the time she was sixteen, she'd kissed a handful of boys. Not enough to make her an expert, by any means. But to fourteen-year-old Jeremy, she had been, and she'd enjoyed playing the role of teacher.

Now, though, they were all grown up and there was no doubt in Bella's mind that the experience level between them had leveled out over the years. Something about that made her a little nervous.

And excited.

She pressed him against the wall and kissed him hard while her hands traveled to his chest.

"This is a very thick jacket." She struggled with the zipper before he cupped his hands over hers and gently removed them.

"Let me." He unzipped his jacket, shrugged it off, and let it land in a heap on the floor. "Better?"

"Not quite." Bella bit her lower lip and once again let her hands roam over his body. This time, her hands slid easily over his thick sweater to the hem, where she could lift it up and over his head.

Damn. He had definitely grown up from the boy he'd been all those years ago.

She swallowed hard and trailed her fingers over the hard planes of his chest. Jeremy shivered under her touch.

"Your hands are freezing." He protested, but made no move to stop her.

His breathing deepened as his chest rose and fell. His arousal fueled her, and Bella moved her hands to his jeans and the undeniable bulge there. Bella ran her hand over his hard-ness and Jeremy groaned. "You're killing me, woman."

"In all the best ways, though."

"Definitely." He bit his bottom lip as she deftly slid the leather from his belt buckle.

Bella took her time unzipping his pants, relishing every moment as she drove him crazier. His breath came faster with every second.

"Bella." He growled her name like a warning. A warning she had no intention of heeding.

With the zipper finally down, she moved her hands—now suitably warmed up—around to his backside and pushed his jeans to the ground. Jeremy stepped out of them and kicked off his boots all in one move, and then he stood before her naked except for his underwear. Bella took a step back to admire the man in front of her. And was there ever a lot to admire.

Jeremy let her look. But only for a moment before he stepped toward her. "Screw this, Bella."

There was only so much one man could take and Jeremy had completely reached his limit. He'd been patient while she undressed him—purposely taking her time to torture him, he was certain. But he let her do it while she herself remained completely clothed. Hell, her winter parka was still zipped up. He'd given her her moment. He'd let her feel as though she were perfectly in charge. Just the way she had been when they were kids. But dammit, by the time she'd stripped him almost completely naked without so much as removing one article herself, he'd reached his breaking point.

"Screw this, Bella."

The half-smile she'd worn on her sexy red lips as she'd taken in her fill of him disappeared as he took two steps toward her and picked her up around the waist, tossing her easily over his shoulder. She squealed in protest, but Jeremy cupped one hand over her ass to hold her in place as he walked across his small apartment to his bedroom.

He flicked on the bedside lamp, giving him just enough light to see the beautiful body he knew she was hiding under all her layers, and tossed her gently onto the bed.

When she looked up at him, the look on her face was one of shock mixed with an overwhelming desire. It took all of his strength not to jump on the bed and rip her clothes off right then.

But no. He wanted to take it slow. He needed to.

Having Bella on his bed, even fully dressed, was quite literally a dream come true. Sure, he hadn't actively fantasized about this moment since he was fourteen—at least, not until lately—but still. It wasn't a moment he was going to rush through.

Hell no.

"You have entirely too many clothes on."

Bella leaned back on her arms. "You didn't really give me a chance to take them off, now did you?"

"Oh, I gave you plenty of time." Jeremy stalked toward the bed and stood at the end, looking down on her. He couldn't touch her. Not yet. "Take off your coat."

She froze, his bossiness catching her off guard.

"Now, Bella."

She hesitated, and for a moment Jeremy wondered whether he'd gone too far. But then a small smile played across her lips; her tongue darted out between them and disappeared just as quickly, leaving him quaking with need but determined to let things play out. With a torturously slow speed, Bella moved her fingers to her zipper and slid it down until she could shimmy out of her parka.

The tight sweater she wore underneath stretched across her breasts as they heaved with the breath she couldn't seem to fully catch.

But he needed more. "And the sweater." Jeremy did his best to look unaffected by her slow motion striptease. But despite his best efforts, he was also aware that his throbbing, incredibly hard erection totally gave him away.

He didn't care.

He swallowed hard as she pulled the sweater up and over her head to reveal full, luscious breasts wrapped in the tiniest slip of lace. Bella's hard, pink nipples stood at attention, begging him to suckle them between his lips.

But not yet.

Bella's breath came in quick bursts as she once more leaned back against her forearms, thrusting her breasts up toward him.

He nodded toward her leggings, but she shook her head in response. "I think I'll need a little help." Her voice was thick with need. "Would you mind?"

As much as Jeremy was enjoying their game, he didn't need to be asked twice. He moved to kneel on the bed and slowly crawled up so he was directly over top of her. He kissed her, pulling her bottom lip between his teeth until she let out a low moan.

Jeremy moved his attentions down her neck, nipping and sucking until he was between her breasts. He inhaled the sweet scent of her, letting it fill him, and then he finally did what every fiber in his body had been yearning for: he moved his mouth over one perfectly plump mound and, through the scrap of lace, sucked her nipple into his mouth.

Bella's body vibrated beneath him. She tilted her neck back and moaned, long and low. Jeremy almost completely lost control at her erotic response. He stilled himself for a moment before turning his attention to her other breast, cupping and massaging the full globes as he went.

Damn.

After a few moments, Jeremy forced himself to keep moving. He trailed kisses down her body until he hit the waistband of her leggings. He slipped his hands past the elastic and moved them down her firm, toned legs, taking the fabric with him, leaving her completely bare. When she was shed of her leggings and boots, Bella reached around her back and unclasped her bra.

She moved backward on the bed, leaned back on her arms and bent her knees, welcoming him to join her.

"God damn, you're beautiful, Bella."

Wanting to keep the situation fair, Jeremy tugged his underwear down and when he stood up again, Bella was licking her lips like a cat about to get her reward.

"You're not too bad yourself, handsome." She crooked her finger, beckoning him to her. "Now get over here and kiss me."

"Yes, ma'am."

Chapter Eight

IT WAS LATE when Bella finally pulled herself from Jeremy's bed. Her body ached all over in the most delicious way as she made her way to the bathroom. Their lovemaking had been... explosive. Bella could have laughed at herself for even thinking it, but there was no other word to describe it. Their coming together had been thirteen years in the making, since those first few fumbling kisses they'd shared when they were kids. And it had been worth every single minute of those years.

Bella took a moment to examine her naked body in the mirror. She'd always been confident about her appearance and her sexuality, but now, as she took in her reflection, it was different. Being with Jeremy had brought out something different in her. She couldn't even begin to explain it, especially because she knew it would sound ridiculous even to her own ears, but she felt as though something had shifted.

Never before had she been with a man who'd worshiped every inch of her body the way Jeremy had. Every touch, every kiss—it was full of...feeling and desire on a level she'd never before experienced.

Bella finished up in the bathroom and crept back into the

bedroom. Jeremy was asleep, but she was too wired to sleep. Not yet. She needed a glass of water, and she should probably check her phone in case her grandfather had tried to call. She hadn't intended to stay out so late. She glanced at Jeremy again. He was sprawled on his stomach, one arm tucked under the pillow, the other outstretched to her side of the bed, where she'd been lying wrapped up in it, only a few moments ago. Her body warmed at the memory. It had been nice to fall asleep with his arm around her, tucked in and protected. *Loved.*

She watched him for another moment before finding her coat on the floor and fishing out her cell phone. Before she left the room, she grabbed a flannel shirt off a nearby chair and as quietly as she could, padded out to the kitchen.

The shirt smelled of Jeremy and it was almost as good as having his arms around her.

Almost.

She helped herself to a glass of water and powered up her phone. The screen lit up almost instantly with dozens of missed texts and calls. But they weren't from Papa.

They were almost all from Kyle. The band leader of her... well, her *former* band.

Where are you?

Gig opportunity of a lifetime.

We need you.

This is everything. The gig. The record deal. Everything. Call me.

Bella scanned the rest of the messages. They were more of the same, increasing in urgency. She dialed into her voicemail. She knew she shouldn't be excited. She shouldn't let Kyle get her hopes up in this way. After all, it was less than a month ago that he'd all but ripped everything away from her.

Well, that wasn't entirely true.

She'd sealed her own fate and had mostly burned that bridge all on her own by freaking out when she'd discovered that he was sleeping with—well, everyone as well as her. Apparently they had different moral and ethical standards. It was true that Kyle had no intention of kicking her out of the band, but it didn't feel right to stay. Not when she'd been played for a fool. At least, that's how it had felt at the time.

Was it worth giving up the increasingly prestigious gigs and the forthcoming record that Kyle kept promising?

Maybe not.

But apparently she hadn't burned the bridge all the way down with Kyle the way she'd been so sure she had.

As she punched in the code for her voicemail, his voice came over the line.

"Bella, baby! You need to call me back right away." He didn't sound upset with her, despite the fact that she'd left him in the lurch for two paid gigs right before running to Glacier Falls. By all rights, he should be livid. But he sounded down-right giddy. "I just got a call from Hector Graham." *Hector Graham?* Why did that name sound familiar? "That name should sound pretty familiar to you, right?" Kyle clearly knew her better than she would have liked. "He's the head of Starshine Records and before you get too excited…" Bella leaned forward in the chair, her stomach twisted in tight knots as she realized exactly who Hector Graham was. "He's not signing us," Kyle continued. Bella sat back. "Not yet." She jumped up from her seat as Kyle's recorded laugh filled her ear. "But he's giving us the chance of a lifetime, baby. A private concert at his house. Just us. We're the opening act and the headliner *and* if it goes well…" Bella held her breath. "That's when we'll get the deal."

Bella wanted to scream. It literally was what she'd been dreaming of her entire life. A deal with Starshine Records was huge. Everyone knew that. She held the phone in front of her, did a silent squeal and danced her bare feet on the tile—careful not to wake Jeremy up, but also way too excited to contain herself. After she got it out, she put the phone back to her ear in time to hear Kyle's recorded voice say, "I hope I can count on you, Bella. It's a group deal. We need you. Just shoot me a text to let me know you're in. We're counting on you."

The call disconnected.

She didn't even have to think about it. Immediately, Bella switched over to her text messaging app and answered Kyle's message.

I'm totally in! OMG!

Unable to contain her excitement for one more moment, she dropped her phone on the table, her water forgotten, and went to wake Jeremy up for a private celebration.

Jeremy yawned. His mouth stretched awkwardly wide, with no hope for covering it. He was on his third coffee of the morning, but it wasn't doing much for his exhaustion.

Not that he was complaining. Not even a little.

Next to him, Natalie gave him a sidelong glance. "Stay up a little too late, did you, Jer?"

"Something like that." He covered his grin with his coffee cup.

"Right." Natalie laughed, the sound filling the cab of the truck. "Your late night wouldn't have anything to do with a certain dark-haired singer who's new to town, would it?"

He didn't bother to deny it.

Jeremy wouldn't trade all the sleep in the world for the night he'd shared with Bella. It had been beyond even his hottest fantasies, and he'd definitely had his share of them. Everything about being with her just…fit. Never before had he felt the way he'd felt with Bella.

Not. Even. Close.

The last thing he'd wanted to do was drop her off at her grandfather's house so he could go to work. But there wasn't much help for it. It's not as if he could call in sick—as much as he wanted to. Christmas Eve was less than twenty-four hours away, which meant there was way too much to do to prepare for Glacier Falls' annual dinner. It had been a tradition started by Ed Walker when he'd first taken over the job as fire chief many years ago. Now, he was getting set to retire, but still the tradition carried on. And as far as Jeremy was concerned, he'd do his best to make sure it did. Even if he didn't get the chief job, which was his ultimate goal.

"We have work to do." Jeremy changed the subject. "We have to pick up the plates and cutlery from the hardware store. They're donating all of it, plus the napkins and some table-cloths. Then we'll get back to the hall and start setting up tables. Last year, there were about eighty for dinner, so we should be prepared for at least a hundred."

"A hundred?"

Jeremy shrugged. "It's not like we're going to turn anyone away and for some reason, it just gets busier and busier."

It was true. What had started out as an event to feed the lonely, disadvantaged, or just those who didn't want to be by themselves for the holidays had bloomed into a potluck of townspeople who simply wanted to share the seasonal spirit with one another. It hadn't been too much of a problem as everyone always brought more than their share of food, and with the local ranchers and farmers donating turkeys and roasts, it didn't cost the department anything except manpower to set it all up. A job Jeremy was happy to take on.

Especially this year. Spending time with Bella had been beyond anything he could have expected. But spending Christmas with her...serving turkey to his friends and neigh-bors...watching her grandfather play Santa for the children...

cuddling up in front of the tree...having his Christmas wish come true...he couldn't think of a better way to spend the next few days.

"There it is again." Natalie interrupted his daydream.

"What?"

"That smile." Natalie shook her head with a laugh. "She's really got you in a twist, doesn't she?"

He didn't bother to deny it. "As long as Bella Burton is the one doing the twisting, I'm completely at her mercy."

Natalie groaned. "You're ridiculous. Just don't let her twist too much, if you know what I mean?"

He didn't.

"Don't get screwed over, Jer," Natalie explained further. "Women like that...well..."

Jeremy bristled and sat up straight behind the steering wheel. "Women like what exactly?"

"Calm down." She shook her head. "All I was going to say is that women like her, who have a career and a life somewhere else, aren't necessarily the best choice to uproot their whole world and move to the middle of the mountains. That's all I was going to say. And weren't you the one telling me that she has a blooming career in music?"

He nodded as what his partner said started to sink in.

"Exactly." Natalie crossed her arms and nodded, her point made. "Glacier Falls isn't really known for its bustling musical scene, is it?" Her lips pressed into a thin line and she shook her head before looking at Jeremy again. She must have seen something in his face, because her approach changed instantly. "I'm not saying that's the case or anything, Jer. It's just I don't want to see you get hurt. You obviously really—"

"It's fine." He held up a hand to stop her. Jeremy didn't know much about Natalie's life before she came to Glacier Falls, but it had been clear early on that she didn't think very highly of relationships or, oddly enough, other women. "I appreciate your concern, but it's not like that. Don't worry."

She gave him a strange look, but thankfully didn't press him further. A fact he was especially appreciative of because he had no idea what he'd even meant by what he said. *It wasn't like what?*

That he was falling for Bella a little more every day?

That he couldn't stop thinking about her? And despite the fact that they hardly even knew each other after ten years, he was very quickly having trouble imagining a life without her in it and that scared the hell out of him?

That as excited as he'd been for her when she'd told him the news about Starshine Records and the gig that was *going to make them,* he was nervous as hell about what that would mean to them, and Natalie's comments had hit a little too close to home?

Because maybe he could lie to Natalie about it, but Jeremy was fairly certain he wasn't going to be able to lie to himself for too much longer.

"Bella, come help me with these presents."

She wiped her hands on the tea towel and dropped it next to the sink where she'd just finished the washing up from lunch, and went to find Papa on his hands and knees under the Christmas tree.

"What are you doing, Papa?" Bella laughed and knelt next to him. "Here, let me get that." She reached past him, flattening herself under the low bough to grab the present he'd been trying to reach.

"What does it look like I'm doing?" With an aching slowness, Papa pushed himself up to standing and promptly sat back on the sofa. "I was trying to get that present."

She went to hand it to him, but he shook his head. "It's for you."

Bella looked from the small package back to her grandfather, a question in her eyes. "It's not Christmas yet."

"I know. But given the exciting news you told me this morning, I thought it was fitting I give it to you now."

Unable to contain herself, as soon as Bella got home that morning, finding her grandfather already up and sitting at the breakfast table with only a raised eyebrow to let her know that he knew exactly where she'd been, she'd told him the exciting news about Velvet Heart and Kyle's voicemail. She'd left a voicemail with Kyle in search of more details about the gig, but so far she'd only received a few vague text messages in return and a promise to give her a call *in a bit*.

"I can wait until—"

"Nonsense," Papa interrupted her. "Open it now. I'm just so proud of you. You've been working hard and now you're going to see your dreams come true. That's a very big deal, Bella. Very big."

There was no way Bella could argue with Papa when he was saying things like that. She turned the package over in her hand and pulled at the tape fastening the shiny paper.

"Just rip it open, kiddo."

Bella laughed and did as she was told. With the paper crumpled and at her feet, she slowly lifted the lid of the box to reveal a delicate, handcrafted silver star-shaped snowflake ornament nestled in the tissue paper.

"Papa. It's gorgeous." Bella gently lifted the ornament by the satin ribbon and held it up. The intricate details of the snowflake sparkled in the light as it twisted from her finger. "I don't know what to say. It's absolutely beautiful."

From his place on the couch, Papa beamed with pride. "It's for my shining star. Bella, you will do great things and this is just the beginning."

A tear came to her eye, but she wiped it away before he could see.

"Hang it on the tree," Papa ordered. "I wanted to see it with the rest of the special ornaments because it will be the last time I get to see a Christmas tree in this house."

Bella froze halfway through hanging the snowflake. Quickly, she finished up, making sure it was secure in the branches before turning to kiss her grandfather on the cheek. "I know it's the right thing, but I can't help but feel a bit sad about it."

"Me too." He nodded and folded his hands over his stomach. "But it's time. You're right and I won't give you any more trouble about it. I'll move."

"You will? Just like that?"

He nodded again. "Just like that. But like I told you before, I'm not going to the city. There's a perfectly good seniors home here in town. Glacier Falls is my home."

She gave Papa a kiss on the cheek. "I know you don't want to leave your house, Papa. But it makes me happy to know you'll be safe. I just want you to be happy."

He smiled and caught her hand in his. "I know, sweet girl. Glacier Falls makes me happy."

After spending more time in town, she could understand that perfectly. Besides, it would give her lots of reasons to come back to visit. *Between Papa and Jeremy, she...* The smile fell from her face. She hadn't let herself think about what her career would mean to her and Jeremy. Not that there *was* a her and Jeremy. But...it sure felt as if there were.

As if he'd read her mind, Bella's phone chirped with an incoming text message. She pulled it out of her pocket and read the message.

Hope you're having a good day. I can't stop smiling.

His honesty put the smile back on her face. She quickly tapped her reply.

Me too. It was a lot of fun.

She was vaguely aware that her grandfather was watching her. "Sorry, Papa. I just—"

"I may be old, but I'm not stupid, child. Go ahead."

She looked back to her phone as it chirped again.

See you tonight? I'll come over.

That was perfect. If Jeremy came over, they'd have the chance to talk about what things would look like when she went back to the city. Long distance wasn't impossible and if they both worked at it, it would work out.

Sounds good.

She'd barely hit Send on her message when the screen lit up with an incoming call. *Kyle.* Finally.

"Sorry, Papa, I need to take this. Kyle is going to give me the details about the gig and—"

He waved her away, and Bella rushed into the kitchen to take the call.

Jeremy pushed the last chair into place and stepped back to admire his work as he felt a pat on his shoulder.

"It looks great, Jeremy."

He turned to see Ed Walker next to him. "Thanks, Chief. It's your vision—I just execute."

Ed laughed. "This is so much more than my vision, son. When I started this dinner all those years ago, there were maybe five people who came. Me and the guys—there were only guys back then—"

Jeremy nodded.

"We roasted a turkey and mashed up some potatoes. That was it. We ate right over there." He pointed to the corner of the station. "Huddled around a card table with a few folding chairs. It was nothing like this, but special nonetheless."

"I bet it was," Jeremy answered honestly. "I'm told Roy Burton was one of those who came that first year." He felt a twinge of sadness that Bella's grandfather had been alone for Christmas after his wife passed.

"It's true." Ed nodded. "It was the first year he'd moved here after his wife died. He'd insisted on staying in town instead of going to visit his family. That was the year we decided Roy would make a good Santa."

"And all these years later, he still puts on that suit." Jeremy smiled.

The two men stood in silence for a few minutes, each lost in their own thoughts before Ed cleared his throat, startling Jeremy. "You'll make a fine chief one day, son."

The comment was unexpected and it took Jeremy off guard. Of course, he hoped to be chief one day; it was his dream and his goal since he was a child. But at twenty-seven, he was too young for the job, wasn't he? There'd been rumors that Ed Walker was getting ready to retire, that he was spending more and more time with a special lady and now that his daughter, Sarah, had married Brody and was settled down again, Ed might just be ready to move on.

But all of that was rumor and hearsay. Jeremy didn't really expect the older man to walk away from his career. Not yet.

He looked at Ed, his face hard to read. "One day, sir. One day."

Ed patted his back and smiled. "One day," he repeated.

***

"I can't do it." Bella walked to the kitchen window and stared out at the snow-covered mountain in an effort to make sense of what Kyle was saying to her.

"You can't—"

"No." She cut him off. "I *can* do it. It's just…"

Shit.

She took a breath and let it out slowly.

"It's just that I didn't realize the gig was tomorrow." Bella dropped her head in her free hand and massaged her temples. *If the gig was tomorrow, that meant...*

"I need you here tonight, Bella. We need to rehearse. I told you in my voicemail." He sighed, that long, exasperated sigh that drove Bella crazy. "I don't understand why you're not already here."

"You didn't say anything about..." She drifted away as she remembered how she'd held the phone away while she celebrated with her little dance in Jeremy's kitchen. It was entirely likely she'd missed some of the finer details of the message. "Shit."

"Exactly, Bella. Shit. I need you to get here right now. How long of a drive is—"

"Two hours, if the weather is good."

"*Two* hours?" Bella could practically see Kyle pacing the floor of his studio apartment where they rehearsed. The vein in his forehead was no doubt pulsing.

She looked out the window again. Blue sky. "If I leave right now, I might be able to get there a bit faster."

But leaving right away would mean missing the Christmas Eve feast. It would mean missing the holiday with Papa. The *last* holiday in his house. It would mean...not saying good-bye to Jeremy.

But it would also mean the biggest opportunity she'd ever had. That she might *ever* have.

It was an impossible choice.

"Get here right away, Bella. I mean it. No more chances after this. I—"

"I got it, Kyle." There was no choice. "I'll be there."

Chapter Nine

BELLA HAD BARELY CAUGHT her breath when Kyle barked out the orders.

"Take it from the top!"

The top?

"Like that last song, or—"

"The top of the set," Kyle interrupted before she could finish the question.

It was a stupid one, anyway. She'd worked with Kyle and the rest of the band for long enough to know how they worked. Hard.

It was how they'd managed to be as successful as they had been so far. And it's exactly why they'd gotten the Christmas gig. They were all perfectionists. It was one of the things that Bella liked most about them all.

But they'd been at it for hours. It was past midnight already. True to her word, Bella had left Glacier Falls right away. She'd taken enough time to talk to Papa, apologizing profusely for leaving him when they had such plans for Christmas in the house. Just the way she knew he'd be, Papa was gracious and supportive. He insisted that she leave right away and *follow her dream.*

"Dreams don't work if you don't, Bella. When an opportunity comes up, you need to take it or you'll spend the rest of your life regretting it."

She'd swallowed back the lump in her throat, taken the bag of food he packed for her while she was throwing her clothes in a bag, and with one last long hug and the promise to come back as soon as she could, she'd left.

"One more," Bella told the guys as she chugged back a bottle of water. "I need to rest my voice if I'm going to be at the top of my game tomorrow."

"And we have a sound check at five," Kyle added. "Which means I want one final run through at nine sharp."

She shook her head a little as she capped the bottle and set it down. But as soon as Bella had straightened and stood up, there was a smile on her face. Her dreams were coming true. This was everything she wanted. And she was going to get it.

As they started the set list again, Bella lost herself in the music. She closed her eyes and poured everything she had into song after song, because she knew if she gave herself the space to start thinking, she'd be lost.

It was the same reason she'd turned her phone to silent and ignored all the text messages and calls from Jeremy. She couldn't allow herself the opportunity to dwell on Glacier Falls, not even for a moment. She needed to focus.

It was the only way.

"She's gone."

Gone.

Bella was gone.

Jeremy replayed the conversation he'd had with Roy earlier

that night at least a dozen times in his head. Maybe more. It still didn't make any sense.

"But she didn't call."

The old man had simply shrugged, but the look on his face was clear. He felt sorry for Jeremy. Or maybe it was for himself.

Bella had left him, too.

But at least he'd gotten to say good-bye.

"I don't understand…"

Jeremy knew he'd sounded like a fool. A weak, twisted up by a woman, fool but he couldn't help it.

Earlier that day, he'd been on top of the world, ready to tell her that he was falling for her. Hard.

And she'd just *left?*

Dammit, he *was* a fool.

He'd made small talk with Roy for a few more minutes, but Jeremy didn't even remember what they'd spoken about except for a brief conversation about how he'd pick the older man up and take him to the firehall for the Christmas Eve dinner the next night. With Bella gone, he'd need a ride and…

"Dammit, Bella." He spoke to his empty apartment and kicked at a shoe that he hadn't bothered to put away.

He'd texted her twice and left two voice messages. His pride wouldn't let him leave any more.

If she wanted to leave without so much as a word to him, well, that was all he needed to know about how she felt. Obviously he'd been wrong about her. Wrong about what they shared and the connection they had. Very wrong.

He should have known something like this would happen. He'd been burned by women before. He should know better than to open up his heart.

But even as he let himself think those things, he couldn't make himself believe them. Bella was different. He just *knew* it. What he had with her…it was *different.*

It didn't matter that it hadn't been long. Time didn't matter. He just needed to...*what?*

Jeremy looked down at the shoe he'd just kicked across the floor.

He needed to go for a run.

After a quick change, Jeremy laced up his shoes, took one last look at his cell phone, and hit the road. It was a clear night and with no cloud cover, it was cold, not that it bothered Jeremy. He pushed his body hard on the icy roads, only vaguely registering that he should be careful. Breaking a leg the day before Christmas wouldn't benefit anyone.

The colorful lights on almost every house and tree cast bright shadows on the snow under his feet as he pressed on, trying to ignore the fact that he'd be celebrating the holiday without Bella.

He ran until he couldn't think anymore. Until all thoughts of Bella, their time together, and her leaving were erased from his brain, replaced only by the basic thoughts of putting one foot in front of the other, inhaling and exhaling as he pushed through the quiet streets of Glacier Falls.

It wasn't until over an hour later when, exhausted, he crawled into bed and closed his eyes that thoughts of Bella once more filled his brain.

Chapter Ten

THE NEXT MORNING, Jeremy needed almost an entire pot of coffee to pull himself together enough to face the day. He'd been up way too late tossing and turning after his run, which had only worked to clear his mind until he stopped moving. The truth was he couldn't turn off his brain and no matter how he tried, he couldn't stop thinking of Bella or what went wrong between them for her to leave without a word.

Sure, Roy said she had a gig with her band. A good one. A career-changing gig. And he would never in a million years begrudge her that opportunity. But she hadn't said good-bye.

And that was the one thing he'd focused on all night until finally, the sun streamed through his window. With the dawning of a new day, he was out of time. He had turkeys to get into the oven at the fire station for dinner later that night, and there was no way he was going to even try to explain why he couldn't get it done this year.

No. There was simply no time for a broken heart on Christmas Eve. Not for Jeremy.

As it turned out, working in the kitchen at the firehall was a great way to put thoughts of Bella out of his mind, and he'd done a great job of hiding any hurt or heartache that he was feeling.

Or so he'd thought.

It wasn't until they got the last bird in the oven, that Stephanie Starz, who'd jumped in with both hands to help out now that she was Glacier Falls' newest resident, turned and snapped a dishtowel at him.

"What's up?" she asked when he gave her a *what the hell* look.

"What do you mean?" He grabbed the empty bowls that had held the bread crumbs they'd used to stuff inside the birds and tossed them in the sink before picking up a rag.

"With you," she said. "What's going on? You seem…"

"Festive?" He made his best effort to grin. "Busy? Overwhelmed with a huge to-do—"

"Sad."

She said it so matter-of-factly, Jeremy decided not to even bother trying to deny it.

"I am." He shrugged and turned his back to fill the sink with hot soapy water. "She left."

"Bella."

It wasn't a question, so he didn't reply.

"It's hard to be involved with someone with a career like hers."

Jeremy turned around, suds on his hands, and looked at his new friend. Not long ago, she'd been engaged to be married in what was supposed to be the wedding of the century according to the tabloids, but at the last minute, had called it off.

"I know a few things about that," she said simply.

He offered her a sad smile. "I guess you do."

Without asking, Steph joined him at the sink. He turned his attention to the dishes, handing each one to her for drying.

"I heard she was offered a pretty big opportunity."

He nodded without asking how she knew. In a small town

like Glacier Falls, it wasn't unusual for word to get around quickly.

"That's what it sounds like."

"Hard to say no to."

He shrugged. "I guess." He handed her a large platter.

"I don't pretend to know what it's like for everyone," she said after a moment. "But I do know that with people like us it's almost impossible to separate your worlds." Jeremy turned to stare at her but she was focused on the plate in her hands. "It's acting for me," she continued. "It's like a drug. Like a pull. I can't not do it. When I'm on set, I feel alive, like I'm doing what I was born to do. Does that make sense?"

He nodded as she finally looked at him.

"I guess it might be like when I'm fighting a fire. It's as if I were meant to be there in that moment, saving that building and saving lives."

Steph smiled. "Exactly. And when you put it that way, your career is far more noble."

"That's ridiculous. It's just different." He shut her down. "The arts are crucial and we all know it. We'd go insane if we didn't have entertainment. It's not better or worse. It's just different."

"Thank you for that."

"I mean it." He handed her a glass bowl.

"Do you understand maybe why she left the way she did?"

Jeremy thought about it for a moment, but finally he shook his head.

"Would you be able to choose?" she asked him. "Between firefighting and her?"

He moved to shake his head, but something stopped him. "It's different."

Her smile was sad, like a woman who knew the answer and knew he was wrong only because she herself had seen more than her share of heartbreak because of a career she loved.

"I never asked her to." His voice was laced with sadness, because he already knew what she was going to say.

"That's the point, Jeremy. You didn't have to."

"That's a wrap, everyone. Go home, get dressed, and see you there at five sharp."

Bella sank into the sofa that had been pushed against the wall of Kyle's studio apartment and dropped her head back, letting her eyes close for a moment. Between the drive through the mountains, the exhausting rehearsal the night before followed by a mostly sleepless night and another morning of rehearsals, she wasn't sure how she was going to keep her eyes open long enough to actually get through the gig later that night.

"I know what you need."

Bella snapped her eyes open at the touch of Kyle's hand squeezing her thigh. Before she could react, he traced a finger up the inside of her leg. She scooted backward seconds before things got even more inappropriate.

"What are you doing?"

"Don't pretend you don't know." His smile was slow and lazy. "This was always your favorite way to unwind after a long rehearsal." He leaned over her and moved to kiss her neck, while his hand cupped her breast, all before she even realized what he was doing.

"Kyle! Stop it." Bella shifted sideways, up and off the couch. "We're not a couple anymore."

He wasn't deterred. "You know that doesn't matter. It was only ever you who was into labels. All I'm saying is a little release always did help you after a rehearsal." He leered at her. "It'll get you ready for the performance tonight. It's a big one. Pretty important, am I right?"

"It is." She couldn't disagree with that fact, but it had nothing to do with sleeping with him. And if he thought for a moment that it did, he was more delusional than she thought.

He stood and walked over to her. It was only then that Bella realized the other band members were already gone. He backed her up against the wall and ran his hand down her arm. "Which is why you need to—"

"Go home and change." She was not about to let him talk her into doing anything that she didn't want to do, or worse—put her into a situation she couldn't get out of. "I was thinking the red, sparkly dress with—"

"That's a good one." He nodded. "But first—"

"No." Bella pressed both palms against his chest and pushed so that Kyle took two stumbling steps backward. "I'm not interested, Kyle. Back off."

"Back off?" He crossed his arms over his chest, his demeanor changing instantly with the rejection. "You've never told me that before."

Bella moved across the room to gather her purse. With every second that passed, she was starting to regret her decision to come back to the city more and more. It had been hard enough to justify leaving the way she did, but now... "You know what? I'm starting to remember why I left the band in the first place."

Kyle laughed. It was a cold, mean sound. When she turned around again, he was shaking his head, an ugly smile on his face. "How could you forget? You had a tantrum, got mad and threw my shit out the window."

"That's because you were—"

"Screwing Dominique," he finished for her. "I thought maybe I could bring out in her what I brought out in you. But, you always were the best, Bella baby."

She cringed at the nickname he'd given her.

"We were dating, Kyle. You cheated on me. And," she

added before turning away, "you didn't bring anything out in me. My voice is my own, and you—"

"Were just a little choir girl who sang along to the radio in her car, when I met you."

She could feel him getting closer, but she didn't turn around.

"You were nothing in this town before you hooked up with me and everyone knows it. You were a timid little church mouse who had no idea how much talent you had inside you just waiting to be brought out. Don't you remember those early days and the way you'd play off how good you were? Now look at you. You're welcome."

She shook her head.

"Yes, Bella. You know it's true. Just like you know that this deal is the best offer you've ever had and it's all because of me. All of your success has been because of me. You'd sink on your own, and we all know it."

She shook her head again and pulled her purse over her shoulder before turning around to face him. He was only inches from her face. When she'd met Kyle years ago, she couldn't get over how handsome he was. His thick, blond hair and his bright-blue eyes. He had surfer looks, but there was a hardness about him, too. An edge that had drawn her to him. And maybe it was true back then that she'd thought she needed him. When she'd started out on the music scene, she was playing at some of the worst bars in town, filling her time by entering contests—like a desperate kid. That's what he'd said to her. At the time, she thought it was true. And maybe even a little funny. After all, Kyle was older and more success-ful. So much more successful. She'd fallen for him and his promises to make her a success.

Looking at him now in a whole new light, it was clearer than ever that she no longer had any feelings for him, and the feelings that she did have before weren't based on anything real and were nowhere near how she felt about Jeremy after such a short time. That was very different.

As far as her success…did she believe that? Maybe some of it. He had given her opportunities. Hell, he was still giving them to her.

She took a deep breath and swallowed hard. "I need to go."

He didn't try to stop her as she stepped around him and walked to the door. With her hand on the doorknob, she hesitated and turned around when he called her name.

"Bella? You look like shit. Put some makeup on before you show up tonight, okay?"

Jeremy couldn't help but smile with Santa sitting shotgun in his truck.

When he'd picked Roy up, he'd expected him to have the suit in a bag to change at the station, but no. He was fully dressed. And more than that, he was in full Santa character from the moment he climbed into the truck next to him.

"You look great, Roy, I didn't even—" The other man shot him a look, so Jeremy quickly amended, "I meant, you look great, Santa."

"Better." Roy chuckled and Jeremy couldn't help but join him.

"Well, you look pretty awesome. And I think you're going to make some kids pretty happy tonight."

"That's why I do what I do, Jeremy. Christmas is about love and happiness."

Jeremy tried not to flinch at his choice of words. He was definitely not feeling either of those things.

"I know what you're thinking."

Jeremy took a second glance at the old man next to him.

"You can't possibly." He shook his head and put the truck in gear.

"Ahh, but you're wrong. I do know." He smiled under his white beard and nodded knowingly. "This time of year, it has a way of being magical, but you have to believe."

"Believe in magic?" Jeremy scoffed. "I don't think—"

"Love," Santa interrupted. "You must believe in love."

With his foot on the brake, Jeremy turned to look at him.

"Take it from an old man who lost the love of his life many years ago. It wasn't always easy, son. But no matter what life threw at us, we pulled through, stronger than ever because of one thing."

"Love?"

The old man nodded. "And here's the thing. Love doesn't always show up the way you want it to. But if you believe, *really* believe, it will be okay. And maybe believing a little bit in the magic of Christmas wouldn't hurt either." He winked and Jeremy could have sworn there was a twinkle in his eye.

He made it sound simple. *Too* simple.

Jeremy stared at the other man for a moment before turning his attention back to the road. He released the brake pedal and navigated through the streets to the station. He made each turn out of habit as his mind tried to make sense of what Roy had just said.

Believe.

He did believe in love. Didn't he?

He thought he did. For a moment, he thought he actually had love. Or at least the start of it with Bella. But…

Maybe he didn't believe.

Or at least not enough.

A few minutes later, he put the truck in park outside the fire station and killed the engine.

Before he could open the door, Santa Roy stopped him. "I'll see what I can do."

"What?" Jeremy shook his head. "You'll see what you can do about what?"

"Your Christmas wish." He winked again at Jeremy and opened the door.

Before Jeremy could stop him or ask him how he even knew what his wish was, the man had slipped out the door and was gone, leaving Jeremy to stare after him.

Chapter Eleven

SHE WAS LATE.

She looked at the glowing lights on her dashboard for what felt like the hundredth time and back outside to the snow-covered pavement ahead of her. It had started snowing at some point during the afternoon while she was in her apartment changing, and it was only coming down heavier with every passing moment.

Bella normally loved a snowy Christmas Eve. But normally, she wasn't late.

It didn't matter how fast she drove—and it couldn't be too fast, given the conditions—she was never going to make it on time.

She tugged at the red sparkly dress, trying in vain to get more comfortable with the skintight fabric wrapped snug around her body. She knew she looked good. Damn good. The dress was the perfect choice for a Christmas Eve gig where all eyes would be on her.

But as a driving outfit…not so much.

She hadn't thought about that when she made the turn off

the freeway that would take her toward the mountains, and away from downtown and the gig that would change her life.

She hadn't thought about much as she'd taken that exit.

Only that it was the right thing to do.

It was the *only* thing to do.

Kyle had been right about one thing: when she'd first started out in her career, she really didn't believe in herself. She had no idea what she was capable of. How talented she was and how far she could go. But he'd been wrong about everything else. She didn't need him to be successful. She never had. That had been her mistake.

She'd forgotten who she was, what she was capable of, and, most critically, what was really important.

That's why she'd taken the exit. Because everything that mattered was two hours away, in the mountains in Glacier Falls. And she was going to be late for the big Christmas Eve dinner at the firehall. But at least she'd get there.

As long as the snowstorm didn't get any worse.

Bella clenched the steering wheel and focused on the road ahead of her. The headlights of the car made the driving snow coming at the windshield look like a scene from a *Star Wars* movie. It was almost impossible to see, but she'd driven in poor conditions before. And there was no turning back now, anyway. Driving through a snowstorm was the least of her troubles. If she didn't get there in time, she'd miss everything. Maybe even her chance to tell Jeremy how she felt.

Assuming she hadn't already missed that chance.

Judging from the piles of dishes, empty platters of food, and the happy laughter all around him, dinner had been a huge success, and Jeremy was exhausted.

He'd smiled and laughed along with his friends and neighbors as he'd served the platters of food. And for a few minutes, when he sat down to eat himself, he'd even managed to forget about Bella and her notable absence.

If his friends had noticed, they mercifully hadn't said anything. Or more likely, Stephanie had briefed them on the situation. For once, he didn't care whether everyone in town knew his business. Not if it kept them from bringing it up out of pity for him. The last thing he felt like was talking about the woman he'd been so sure had been more than a holiday fling.

Fortunately, the conversation centered around what everyone else was up to. Hope and Levi's plans for the baby who was due in a few months, the winter weddings that were to be held for the first time at Ever After Ranch, how Brody Morris and his new wife Sarah were going to handle the increase in business from catering the wedding and running Birchwood restaurant. Sarah's daughter, Rory, chimed in that her Christmas wish was a little baby brother or sister, and everyone laughed—except Brody and Sarah, who stared at each other with wide eyes. Stephanie told the group about some scripts she was entertaining and then shocked everyone when she casually mentioned that she'd bought the old fishing camp on the edge of town. She wasn't sure what she was going to do with it yet, but it was going to be *perfect*.

Jeremy could only shake his head and laugh because he had no doubt that it would be. Stephanie had a way about her of making things work out *perfectly*.

He excused himself as Damon started to talk about some new investments he was considering.

He loved his friends, but pretending was getting harder by the moment. What he really needed was a shot of whisky and a reality check. Bella had only been back in his life for a few weeks, hardly anything he should let ruin the holidays. Better to know where he stood early on before he invested too much time, only to have his heart broken later.

At least, that was the advice he'd give a friend. Too bad he didn't believe it.

"You did a great job tonight, Jeremy." Katie appeared next to him in the kitchen with a stack of dishes.

"Thanks." He turned away, busying himself putting cling wrap over the leftover platters. "That means a lot."

"Are you okay?"

He stopped. Katie was probably the last person he wanted to talk to about how he was feeling. Sure, she probably knew him the best out of anyone, given their on-again/off-again relationship since high school, but that was also why it felt strange. Besides, he'd just started to do a good job fooling himself that it was all for the best that Bella had left. Or at the very least, he was trying to fool himself and that had to count for something.

"I'm sorry she left," Katie said before Jeremy could answer. "But that doesn't mean—"

"I don't want to talk about it." He shut her down before it could go any further.

But Katie was not one to be deterred easily. "Yeah, I got that. But maybe you should."

He turned to look at her then. There was nothing but care and concern on her face. "Katie, really, I—"

"Look." She held up a hand to stop him. "I'm not going to force you. All I'm going to say is that sometimes things aren't as black and white as you'd like them to be. There's a whole lot of gray in life, Jeremy. And take it from someone who knows— sometimes it's hard to see through all of that gray to what's really in front of you. It's not always that straightforward, that's all I'm saying."

He let her words sink in and, to his surprise, didn't reject them out of hand. He nodded slowly but didn't offer anything more.

"Don't hide in here all night, okay?" She gave him a quick kiss on the cheek before heading for the door. He watched as she turned around again. "It's Christmas. And you never know what the magic of Christmas can bring."

She was gone before she could see him groan and shake his head.

It was later than she thought by the time Bella pulled into Glacier Falls. Dinner would certainly be over by now. She almost steered the car toward her grandfather's house and the warm familiarity she'd most certainly find there. But she wouldn't find what she needed there.

It only took a few more minutes to get to the firehall. She had to park down the street and pick her way through the icy and snowy sidewalk toward the festivities. She could hear the music and laughter as soon as she stepped outside the car. It was a sound that made her both excited and terrified at the same time.

She knew that Papa would be happy to see her, at least until he learned that she'd blown off the gig that could have potentially been the catalyst to a huge career. He'd be disappointed to hear that. After all, she was supposed to be his shining star. The one that followed her dreams and made everything come true.

Bella swallowed down the lump of uncertainty.

She'd made the right decision. She knew that. She felt it.

After she'd left Kyle's apartment, she'd gone home, showered, carefully done her hair and makeup, and slipped into the sexy dress. She looked amazing and, judging by their earlier rehearsals, she sounded amazing. It was all lining up to be a perfect night. The night that would launch their careers and secure them the record deal with Starshine Records. It was everything she'd always wanted.

But it wasn't.

She couldn't shake the feeling that it was wrong. All of it. It felt wrong. It *wasn't* everything she'd ever wanted. The feeling had only grown stronger as she started to drive until she took the exit that led to the mountains and Glacier Falls. The minute she'd pointed her car in the *right* direction, the weight had started to lift.

Papa would be disappointed, that was certain. But Bella knew as soon as she explained her reasons to him, he'd understand. Besides, this was far from the end of her career. No matter what Kyle's angry voicemails and text messages said. He was wrong about her. Always had been. And there was no way she would ever feel good about moving ahead with her career if it was any way linked with him. Those days were over.

Bella stood in front of the door to the firehall and took another deep breath. She had no idea what waited for her inside. Whether Jeremy would even speak to her, let alone forgive her for leaving the way she had. She wasn't sure she could. But she hoped with her entire heart that he would.

And even if he didn't, she needed to try. Bella was done hiding from what she really wanted. Papa had spoken to her about following her dreams and going after the thing she really wanted.

She wanted Jeremy. She had no idea what that looked like or even what it meant, but she wanted him with a ferocity inside that she couldn't deny. It seemed impossible in such a short time, but she was falling for him. Heck, she'd already fallen for him.

With one last deep breath, she tossed her hair over her shoulder and pulled the door open.

Katie was right. Jeremy hated to admit it, but she'd been right. At least about one thing. After she'd left him alone in the kitchen, he'd wrapped up two more platters of leftovers before he'd had enough and left the rest of the mess in the kitchen for the others to handle. It was Christmas, after all, and even if it wasn't going exactly the way he'd hoped it would, all of his friends were there and he was going to enjoy himself...even if it killed him.

He poured himself a drink and joined the rest of the group, who were passing out song books and singing along to the band who'd started up in the back of the hall.

Maybe it was because he'd most recently done it with Bella tucked up next to him on the sleigh ride a few days ago, but something about singing Christmas carols made him smile.

And that's just what he was doing when "*Away in a Manger*" finished.

"See?" Katie elbowed him. "There's that smile. That's all I wanted to see."

Jeremy turned around so he could face all his friends. "Here it is." He grinned widely for them all and raised his glass. "Merry Christmas, everyone. I'm really glad you are all—"

"Chestnuts roasting on an open fire."

He froze, his glass in midair.

There was only one voice that sounded like an angel.

Bella.

His friends, the noise, the room full of people faded away as Jeremy turned slowly to see Bella on the stage, the microphone in her hand, as though she were born to be there. She was absolutely stunning in a fitted red dress that hugged every one of her curves and sparkled under the Christmas lights that hung over the stage. Her long, dark hair hung in soft waves over her shoulders and her piercing green eyes looked directly at him as she sang the lyrics to the familiar Christmas song. Just as she had days earlier at Ever After Ranch.

Despite being surrounded by almost a hundred of his friends and neighbors, this performance was dramatically more intimate. Everyone else fell away and it was just the two of them. She sang directly to him. The familiar lyrics of his favorite carol had never sounded so romantic, so special, and so completely perfect.

It wasn't until the last chorus that Jeremy even realized he was up and out of his seat. He made his way through the crowd until he was on the stage standing next to Bella as she sang the last line, "Although it's been said many times, many ways…Merry Christmas, to you."

She reached out her hand and he took it. The crowd erupted in applause as he pulled her to him and kissed her, long and slow.

He could have kissed her forever, and he planned to. But first, there was something he needed to say. "Bella, I—"

"Jeremy, I'm so—"

He silenced her with a gentle finger to her lips. She had a lot of explaining to do, of that there was no doubt. But there would be time for that.

"Later," he whispered. "Right now, the only thing that matters is that you're here and I'm here with you in my arms. I don't know if it's the magic of the season or what, but what I do know, Bella Burton, is that I'm falling in love with you."

Her smile was the sweetest and sexiest thing he'd ever seen all at once, but when she spoke, he knew he was gone for good. Bella bit her lower lip. "I can't tell you how glad I am to hear that, Jeremy, because I've already fallen. Completely and totally. I love you."

Jeremy didn't care that everyone was watching and even that the applause had turned into cheering as he kissed her again, this time deeper. He didn't care because the only thing that mattered was that she was there. She was in his arms, she felt the same way he did, and his Christmas wish had come true.

Chapter Twelve

WHEN BELLA WOKE up with Jeremy's arm snuggled around her, holding her close against his hard chest, she contemplated pinching herself to see whether it was true. Because how could it be?

She'd made such a mess of things. To the point that she wasn't sure she could salvage things. But not only had she, but...it had been the most perfect night.

When she'd walked into the firehall the night before, she hadn't seen him among the crowd, and her stomach had dropped. She'd missed him. But then she saw Santa with that familiar twinkle in his eye, and she went to him.

Bella didn't dare to hug him, lest she fall apart right there in front of the entire town. Instead, she sat next to Papa and took his white gloved hand in hers. "I'm sorry. I couldn't do it."

"It wasn't right, Bella."

She looked at him and tried to read his eyes. *How could he know what the situation was?* She hadn't said a word except to lie to him about how great the band was and how awesome Kyle was. She regretted that now. Like so many other things.

"But it will be." He squeezed her hand. "Fate had other plans for you this Christmas."

She narrowed her eyes in question.

"Perhaps it wasn't right this time because you had more important things to take care of right here?"

"But you told me to follow my dreams."

He smiled, his beard twitching up. "I also told you that there's always more than one path to get where you're going, and if you aren't paying attention you could miss the path that will change everything, remember? Sometimes life has a way of working out that you wouldn't expect and that you'd never experience if you didn't keep your eyes and your heart open to it."

She thought about what he'd said for a moment.

"But what if it's too late?" It *was* too late. Jeremy was gone already, and she hadn't had the chance to tell him how she really felt.

Papa winked and nodded his head to the right. Bella followed his gaze as he said, "It's never too late."

And it hadn't been. The band was more than happy to help her out with her song choice. The moment she stepped out there with the microphone in her hand and started singing directly to Jeremy, she poured everything she had into the performance that was just for him.

The rest of the night had gone by in a blur. There had been hugs and well wishes, Merry Christmases and even a few congratulations, but through it all, Jeremy had been right there at her side and that was all that mattered.

He was there. She was there. And they loved each other.

She looked over her shoulder. He was still asleep. As much as she didn't want to leave the warmth of his embrace, she was also very aware that it was Christmas morning and Papa would be up soon. As quietly as she could, she tried to slip from the bed.

Jeremy's arm tightened in response. "Where do you think you're going?" He pulled her back into his embrace and kissed her neck.

A small sigh slipped from her lips, but she needed to be strong. "I need to get up. It's Christmas."

"More the reason to stay in bed." He flipped around and was over top her, framing her with his strong arms so quickly, she didn't have time to react. "I want to give you your Christmas present." He dipped his head and started to kiss her chest, working his way down her body.

The temptation was strong.

"You gave me my present last night." His head popped up over top her once again. "And I enjoyed it very much."

"As did I." His grin was wicked. "So much so, it's time for another."

She laughed. "Later. I want to get breakfast started for Papa. It's Christmas."

His eyes grew wide. "You're cooking?"

She narrowed her eyes.

"In that case, I better get suited up with a fire extinguisher. I mean, I've seen what you can do to an innocent lasagna."

She smacked his chest lightly, rolled out from under him, and swung her bare legs over the edge of the bed. "It's a good thing I did burn that lasagna," she said as she reached back to pull her hair into a ponytail. "Or we might not have met again."

She moved to stand, but before she could, Jeremy's strong arms were pulling her back down to the bed and into his lap, where he kissed her hard. "Babe, our paths would have crossed no matter what you burned." He kissed her again. "You were my Christmas wish, after all."

It had been the best Christmas Jeremy could remember. After an easy breakfast—where no one burnt anything—they'd video chatted with Jeremy's parents and sister. They were all thrilled to meet Bella virtually and were excited to meet her properly when they returned from their trip. They hadn't discussed what their next step was, or whether Bella would be returning to the city right away, but this time Jeremy knew they would talk about it and whatever they decided, they would decide together. There were sure to be some hard decisions, but Jeremy was confident they could face anything life threw at them as long as they did it together.

They opened the few presents there were, and spent a lazy afternoon working on jigsaw puzzles and watching Christmas movies. Roy even let them discuss the seniors homes he'd consider moving into, and Jeremy happily agreed to help out by taking him on any tours or visits if Bella or her mom couldn't make it. Jeremy could tell that the older man didn't want to admit it, but he looked more than a little excited about the prospect of moving. Especially considering they'd just heard that his next-door neighbor, Lydia Arthur, was also considering a move. The twinkle in Roy's eye when he got the news confirmed what Jeremy had long suspected—there was more than a neighborly interest there.

Bella had just started to drift off, her head on his shoulder, when Roy stood up from his easy chair and announced it was time to get ready.

"For what?" Bella sat up, awake again.

"Dinner." Roy looked at her as though she were crazy. "It's Christmas. We have to have dinner."

"Papa, I'm sorry. I didn't even think of dinner." Bella shook her head. "I didn't prepare anything. I don't even know if we have—"

"Nonsense. We're not cooking." Roy laughed, clearly happy to have fooled his granddaughter. "We were invited to the

Langdon ranch for dinner. Well, I was, anyway. But I assume that invitation will be extended."

Jeremy wiggled his eyebrows at the old man, who only chuckled.

"Debbie Langdon is young enough to be my daughter. We're old friends is all. And she's a nice lady who took pity on an old man alone on Christmas." He shook his head and muttered as he shuffled from the room to get ready. "Damn kids, thinking everything is more than it is."

As soon as he left, Bella looked up at him with tired eyes. "I'm so exhausted," she said. "I don't know if I can do it."

He hugged her tight, afraid she might actually cry from exhaustion. "We don't have to go," he said in her ear. "I'll drive Roy over and come back and make us grilled cheese. It's Christmas. We don't have to—"

"Exactly. It's Christmas." She forced a smile. "They're your friends."

"And yours." He kissed her gently. "Which is why they'll understand, Bella. It's okay. We just saw them last night. It'll be fine. I promise."

Jeremy wasn't surprised when, forty minutes later, after he'd deposited Roy on the Langdon ranch, gave everyone his best wishes and made his apologies for him and Bella and finally returned to Roy's place, the house was quiet. Bella was fast asleep on the couch. He pulled an afghan over her and went to the kitchen to, as quietly as he could, prepare a grilled cheese holiday feast.

The smell of the toasting bread must have woken her because as Jeremy was setting the table, Bella appeared in the doorway. She yawned widely and grinned. "It smells amazing in here."

He held out the platter of sandwiches with a flourish. "Nothing but the best for our first Christmas together."

"It's absolutely perfect." Bella sat at the table. "I hope they weren't too upset about us bailing on dinner."

"Not even a little bit. They totally understood. But Stephanie sent a card home for you. Hold on."

He grabbed the card for her to read while he continued to set the table. It was only after he'd opened the bottle of wine that he realized Bella hadn't said anything for a few minutes. He turned to see her holding the Christmas card in one hand, a business card in the other, her mouth wide open.

"What is it? Is everything okay?"

She nodded slowly but still didn't speak, so Jeremy took the card from her and read:

Bella,

You have the most amazing voice I've heard in a very long time and I know you will be absolutely perfect for this script I'm reading. This is my agent's card. He's expecting your call and after I sent him the video I recorded last night, even more excited about your future than I am.

Merry Christmas.

Steph

"Holy shit." Jeremy finished reading the card and looked at Bella, who had tears streaming down her face. "Right?"

She nodded. "I don't know what to say. Why is this happening?"

Christmas feast forgotten, Jeremy wrapped her up in his arms and spun her around the kitchen. "You don't have to say anything, Bella. You deserve this and I can't believe I'm saying this, but it's all just the magic of Christmas at work."

That made her laugh. "You're a crazy man."

"Maybe so." He kissed her. "But I'm *your* crazy man. Merry Christmas, Bella."

Thank you so much for reading *We Wish You A Happily Ever After*!
I hope you loved meeting Bella and Jeremy. But their story is far from over...Keeping Happily Ever After is next in the series. You can read a sneak peek of Chapter One, next!

In the meantime, if you love small town romances, you'll love my series, The McCormicks. And you can download the first in the series for FREE!
Read on for a preview of Love in the Moment!

Make sure to sign up for my newsletter so you'll be the first to hear when a new story is released!
You can join me here —>
https://elenaaitken.com/newsletter/

Keeping Happily Ever After

Please enjoy this excerpt from the upcoming Keeping Happily Ever After
Available Spring 2021

IT WAS COLD. Really cold. The type of cold that froze your eyelashes to your face the moment you set foot outside. Which was exactly why a rookie should have been the one heading to the grocery store in the deep freeze, instead of Jeremy Davis. But when the fire chief gave you an order, you didn't pass it off. Even to a rookie. Even when it was absolutely ridiculous that Jeremy had to be the one to go to the grocery store that afternoon to pick up fresh rosemary, of all things.

The saving grace in the entire situation was that Ed Walker, the fire chief, was an amazing cook and if he wanted fresh rosemary, it meant there was going to be pot roast on the menu that night. Jeremy's mouth watered at the thought. Most of the firefighters had become good cooks over the years out of necessity, but Ed was by far the best. Likely because he'd been at it the longest, which was also why the rumors were only heating up that Ed was getting ready to retire and appoint a new chief. A role that Jeremy had been working toward since he'd joined the Glacier Falls fire department seven years ago as a rookie himself.

In a small mountain town like Glacier Falls, the department hadn't been very big even when Jeremy had joined. But over the last few years, they'd grown, along with the town, and even though at only twenty-seven, Jeremy might still be considered a rookie, he was ready for the challenge of a growing fire department.

"But first," he muttered to himself as he steered the department pickup truck down the icy street, "rosemary."

He was just about to take the turn into the grocery store lot when his radio crackled to life.

"Davis, possible sparks detected over at Burton's place," the voice said.

Shit.

He was only half a block away. Even without the rig, he was the logical dispatch. "10-4," he said quickly into the radio. "On my way."

Jeremy flicked his light on, shoulder checked and quickly changed course.

He'd been hoping there wouldn't be another call out to Roy Burton's place before they managed to move the elderly man into the retirement home he'd finally agreed to. Especially because Jeremy knew he was in the house alone. Before Christmas, the fire department had responded regularly to calls at Roy's house. Thankfully, that had changed after Bella, Roy's granddaughter, came to town for the holidays and convinced him it was time to move.

But Bella, Jeremy knew, wasn't with her grandfather at the moment. She'd returned to the city for a few weeks and wasn't due back for two days, ten hours, and four more minutes.

And although it would be safer for Roy to have Bella back

in town, Jeremy was far more concerned with himself and how great it would be to have her back in his arms once again.

And his bed.

Jeremy shook his head to clear it as he pulled up in front of Roy's house. He would allow himself to think about Bella later. First things first: making sure Roy was okay and hadn't set his kitchen on fire. Again.

He moved quickly, grabbing a fire extinguisher from the back seat before running up the steps and banging on the door. "Roy?" He knocked again. "Roy, you in there?"

Without waiting for an answer, Jeremy tried the door handle. And just as it always did, the door opened freely. He stepped across the threshold and called out again. "Roy?"

Jeremy sniffed the air for smoke. Nothing.

He scanned the room. Nothing seemed out of place.

And then a flicker of movement caught his eye. He turned and subsequently froze as his brain registered what he was seeing.

"Bella?"

The most beautiful woman he'd ever seen leaned against the doorframe that he knew led to a small bedroom. Her long, dark, wavy hair cascaded over her bare shoulder. Jeremy let out a low whistle as he took in the sight of the woman he was very rapidly falling in love with, wearing nothing more than a red silky negligee and a wicked smile on her face.

But he needed to focus.

"Roy? Is he—"

"Fine." Bella stepped toward him. "Safely next door with Lydia."

Jeremy's brain was having trouble keeping up. "So there are no sparks?" As he said it out loud, he realized it was a ridiculous call. Never in his career had he ever been called out for *possible sparks*.

Now, only inches away, Bella reached out for the collar of

his jacket and pulled him toward her as she shook her head. "Not yet," she whispered against his mouth. "But hopefully soon there'll be a few."

It wasn't until she pressed her sensuous lips to his and kissed him fully that Jeremy allowed himself to believe what he was seeing was real. *Bella. In his arms.* Earlier than two days, ten hours, and four more minutes.

He broke the kiss long enough to set the fire extinguisher down, and scoop Bella up so he could carry her down the hall into her bedroom.

"Tell me again." Jeremy shook his head and laughed. "How did you make this happen?"

It had been less than two weeks since Bella had left Glacier Falls for the city. Barely enough time to take care of the meetings she had scheduled with her new agent and casting directors that her new friend, the mega celebrity Stephanie Starz, had introduced her to after hearing Bella sing. They had been a very exciting few weeks as she sang for more people than she could remember and even ran lines, something she'd never considered doing. But even though she'd been so busy she barely had time to sleep, she'd still had a lot of time to miss Jeremy terribly. Which was why she'd decided to return to town earlier than planned. Definitely a good decision, judging by the smile on Jeremy's face as he laid on his side, propped up on a pillow, the bed sheet slipping just a little off his hip. Yes. She'd definitely made the right decision to come back early.

"I knew you had to work," Bella explained for the third time. "So I called in a favor with the chief. He's still pretty pleased with me for singing at the Christmas Eve dinner." She grinned and then squealed as Jeremy reached out and pulled her on top of him.

Her squeals quickly dissolved into satisfied moans as he wrapped his arms around her and kissed her deeply again. They'd just finished making love and reacquainting themselves with each other, but that didn't seem to matter to Jeremy. Or her. Except for the fact that she'd promised her grandfather they'd start packing later that afternoon.

Besides the fact that Papa could come home at any time from Lydia's, she really was pushing it by laying here naked with Jeremy. As much as she was enjoying every second of it.

Reluctantly, she pushed herself up from his chest. "We can't," she protested. "We don't have time. My grandfather will be home anytime."

"One more kiss." He pulled her back down onto him, and she couldn't bring herself to protest as his hands slid up her bare back.

In fact, ten minutes later, she still wasn't protesting, but was participating fully in his distraction techniques when they both heard the front door open.

"Shit." Jeremy jumped up like a teenager caught by his girl-friend's parents and grabbed at a pillow to cover his naked body with.

Bella couldn't help it; she burst out laughing and only belatedly slapped a hand over her mouth to stifle her giggles. A technique that didn't work very well as the laughter slipped out between her fingers when Jeremy started dashing around the room, looking for his clothes.

"Bella! This isn't funny."

"It is, though." She tried to swallow her laughter, but failed. "It really is." She probably could have laughed at him all after-noon, but the genuine horror on his face when he couldn't find his pants spurred her into action. "Okay, fine."

It's not as if they were going to go back to cuddling, anyway. She might as well help him out.

It only took Bella a few seconds to gather his clothes,

pulling his pants from the twisted quilt at the foot of the bed, and tossing them toward him. "Honestly, Jeremy. It's okay. He gets it. He does."

Jeremy shook his head and quickly pulled his pants on before tugging his sweater into place. "Easy for you to say. You're his sweet, perfect granddaughter who can do no wrong. I'm just the guy sleeping with her."

His choice of words stopped her and she turned to look at him halfway through tugging her leggings on. "That's it? You're just the guy sleeping with me?" She didn't want it to, but his nonchalance bothered her. More than she thought it might. After all, they had only been together since Christmas. Less than a month. They weren't serious. The words girlfriend and boyfriend were barely even used. In fact, they hadn't really discussed anything serious about their relationship and—

"No." He interrupted her train of thought. Thankfully before her thoughts could spiral too far in a negative direction. Jeremy knelt in front of her and grabbed her hands, forcing her to focus on him. "That is definitely not all I am, babe. I am *so* much more than that. At least I want to be. You know that."

She nodded and her smile was genuine. "I do."

"Good." Jeremy leaned in to kiss her. "In fact…I would really like to be—"

"Bella?"

Jeremy jumped up at the sound of her grandfather's bellow, causing Bella to laugh again.

"One minute, Papa. I'll be right there."

She quickly finished getting dressed. "Can we finish this conversation later?"

"That's a promise." He kissed her again, and Bella melted into it the way she always did.

She forced herself to pull away from him again. Something that was becoming harder and harder to do. "Come on. Let's go say hi." Bella took his hand and led him out to the living room. She'd only been back with Jeremy for a few hours, and already the idea of being away from him again was getting harder and harder to fathom.

And that was a problem. A big problem. Because those meetings she'd had in the city had been very promising. And if everything went according to plan, and the way she hoped, she was going to be spending a lot more time away from him.

Bella snuck a glance at Jeremy as he greeted her grandfather with a hug.

Or, she was going to have a very big decision to make.

Either way, she wasn't looking forward to it.

Love in the Moment

PLEASE ENJOY **an excerpt from the first book in my bestselling series, The McCormicks! Right now you can download Love in the Moment for FREE!**

Ian McCormick stole a glance at the woman sitting next to him. He'd picked her up only ten minutes earlier from the bus station and already he'd run out of things to talk about. In fact, beyond the general introductions they'd exchanged, they really hadn't spoken at all. He felt as if he should say something to break the silence, but every time he opened his mouth, he drew a blank. What was he supposed to say to the younger half-sister he'd never met?

The sister that he'd never had any desire to meet, not since finding out about her existence almost ten years ago. As far as he was concerned, Ian could have gone the rest of his life without knowing about Chelsea or her sister, Amber's existence. And he really didn't see any need to get to know either of them. After all, they were the reason his entire life had imploded all those years ago.

Okay, that wasn't entirely fair. It wasn't their fault that their father had led a secret life, with a completely different family. A family he'd finally left his *other* family for, leaving Ian, his brothers, and his mother all alone. *No. It wasn't the girls' fault.* But all of the reasoning in the world hadn't made it any easier for Ian to wrap his head around it. Despite the fact that it had been almost a decade ago.

He snuck another look at the girl who had barely looked up from her phone since she'd sat down in the jeep. There was definitely a family resemblance. She had their father's green eyes, just like he did. And the dark, thick hair. He hated to admit it, but there was no denying she was his sister. And it wasn't as if he could spend the whole summer not talking to her. He'd made a promise to Declan, his second youngest brother.

"It's not her fault," Declan had said on the phone. *"Chelsea and Amber aren't to blame, Ian. You need to get over it."*

Dec was right. He did need to get over it, especially since she was going to be staying with him all summer. He took a breath and opened his mouth to say something, but didn't have a chance.

"I know you hate me."

Ian shut his mouth dumbly.

"And I suppose you think you have a reason to," Chelsea continued. "But it wasn't my idea to come here, you know? Declan pretty much insisted that it would be *good for me* or something, and…well…I kinda trust Dec. Besides, I didn't really have anywhere else to go."

He swallowed hard, giving himself a moment. "I don't hate you." As he spoke the words, he realized they were true. "I just don't know you. And Declan's right. It will be good for you here."

"You don't even know why he said that."

"I don't need to." Ian slowed the jeep to take the turn that would lead them out of town, toward the cottages. His house sat at the end of a row of other log cabins that were used primarily by summer people. Most of the houses were built by families who came from the city for the summer months, and they were still locked up tight because the season wouldn't start for another month or so. It was quiet, but Ian liked it. At least for now, while he was getting settled. And it was true, he didn't know why Declan thought it was a good idea for Chelsea to get out of the city for the summer, but he had a few guesses, and there was no doubt that a little bit of quiet would be good for her, too. "I trust Declan, too," he said as the jeep bumped over the dirt road. It was impossible not to trust Declan. Out of all of his siblings, Dec was definitely the most trustworthy, and the most compassionate and caring and...he was pretty much everything good in the world. "If he thinks it'll be good for you out here, he's probably right."

She shrugged and turned back to her cell phone, looking up a moment later in horror. "The service is terrible here."

"One of my favorite features." He smiled.

"Why would that be a good thing?"

He ignored the question. "It's not that bad, really. Just a little spotty sometimes. Besides, you'll be able to get Wi-Fi at the Dockside as soon as I get it hooked up."

"The Dockside?"

"The new marina." Ian couldn't help but smile. "Cool name, right?" The main reason he'd returned to Cedar Springs was because the economy was starting to pick up, and there were business opportunities to be had. One of the first he'd found was the old marina. It was just next to the Grizzly Paw on the beach in town and Ian remembered it as *the* meeting place for summer fun. He picked it up for a bargain basement price, probably because it needed so much work. By the looks of things, it had sat empty for years and it would definitely take a little elbow grease to get it up and running again. Not that

Ian was afraid of hard work. In fact, that had always been his favorite part of a new business: turning nothing into something. "I just closed on it yesterday. And with any luck, it will be open and ready for business in time for the season to start. But if that's going to happen, I'm going to need a little help."

She looked at him sideways. "And I suppose you want me to help."

"You got it. Call it...the price of admission."

She rolled her eyes and shoved her phone into her duffel bag. "Why not? I guess a summer job won't hurt."

"Oh no." Ian braced himself for her response to what he was about to tell her. "Helping at the marina isn't a summer job—it's just an expectation. I got you a job, too. You'll be starting at the Grizzly Paw right away. Sam's an old friend of mine, and she's doing me a favor by giving you this job, so I know you won't let me down."

"Two jobs?"

"No." He shook his head. "Just one. And a family project."

"But I'm never going to have any time to have fun," she wailed.

That was the point, at least as far as Ian was concerned. He didn't know much about twenty-two-year-old girls, but from what Declan had told him, Chelsea was making far too many poor choices. And as the big brother—whether he wanted to be or not—it was going to be his job to help her make good ones. Or keep her too busy to make anything but.

When Gwen Henderson had dreamed of her triumphant return to Cedar Springs after years of hard work and sacrifice, she'd dreamed of driving an expensive convertible down Main Street, her dark hair floating in the breeze as all the men's heads turned to see the beautiful and famous celebrity she'd turned out to be as they kicked themselves for not dating her when they had their chance.

Yes, in her fantasies, it was perfect. In reality, however, she had not imagined that on the eve of her summer visit to Cedar Springs, her secondhand Mustang would have some random, and likely expensive, engine problem that would require her taking the bus into town. And she most certainly did not expect that the one man who'd not only turned her down as a teenager, but had publicly humiliated her ten years earlier at the Summer Equinox Festival, would be there when she got off the bus.

Ian McCormick.

He didn't even *live* in Cedar Springs. What were the odds the one man who still haunted—no, not haunted...*visited*—her dreams would not only be standing there when she got off the stupid, humiliating bus, but would also look her square in the eye and not even recognize her?

If she was honest with herself, and she'd made that a habit over the last few years, that was the part that hurt the most. Ian McCormick had been her biggest teenage crush. No, her *only* teenage crush. Every summer for four years, she had lusted after him. Practically threw herself at him that final summer. But he'd barely even noticed her and when she thought she'd finally had a date with him at the festival, he'd stood her up. Left her there all alone. She knew now he'd only said yes to the date out of pity. After all, it didn't make sense for someone as handsome and smart as Ian McCormick to go out with fat, pimple-faced, four-eyed, frizzy-haired *Giant Gigi*. At the time, she'd been heartbroken—totally destroyed, really. But time and distance had taught her social order. The other thing time and distance had taught her was the impact that health, fitness, contacts, clear skin, a new hair-do, and a name change could do for social order.

It had been five years since she'd dropped the stupid childhood nickname, adopted a fitness regime and lost seventy-five pounds, finding herself and a new career in the process. Early on in her transformation, Gwen decided to document everything on social media, using a blog and then a Facebook and Instagram account to chronicle her progress. The result was not only a whole new body, but also a very loyal following, commercial and marketing deals, and the potential for a book and maybe even a reality television show. She was a very different person than the sad, overweight teenager she'd been on her summer visits to see her grandma in Cedar Springs. *Very* different. And with women looking up to her and men lining up to date her, she no longer needed Ian McCormick to validate her worth.

But if that was true, why had her heart done a stupid little flip when he'd grabbed her bag at the bus stop? And why had her pulse raced out of control when he looked at her? How was it even possible that he could still have that effect on her after all these years?

"Gwen!"

Deanna Gordon shot out of the building across the street and without even looking, raced across the street and pulled her into a hug. "Oh my goodness, you look amazing." Deanna held her out at arm's length for a fraction of a second before she pulled her back into a hug. "I'm so glad you're finally here. I was going to meet you at the bus stop—that's crazy that your car broke down—but I got caught up with a patient and—"

"It's okay." Gwen finally cut her off with a laugh. "I literally only walked half a block. Don't worry about it."

Deanna bent down and scooped up her bag. "Is this all you have? One duffel bag? I don't think I could travel that light if I tried."

Gwen laughed again. "Are you kidding? The rest of my bags are coming later. I may have sweet-talked the guy at the depot to deliver them personally."

"You did not?"

She only smiled in response. It wasn't often that Gwen used her curves and killer smile to get her way, but sometimes she couldn't seem to help herself. Besides, it's not as though she did it very often.

Deanna shook her head, but her friend smiled. "Hey, if you can get away with it…why not, right?"

"Exactly. And heaven knows I haven't always had this skill. I might as well take advantage sometimes. But don't tell anyone, okay?"

Deanna stared at her. "Who would I tell?"

She forgot sometimes that not everyone lived their whole life online. For Gwen, it was normal to record everything, and censor anything she didn't want getting out. It was a carefully constructed existence, one that was almost entirely public, because she'd built her following by *not* keeping very much private. Her readers liked to hear everything about her, including her workouts, what she had for dinner, her dates, and even more personal things about her dating habits. Not that she'd had much to report lately. She may get a lot of attention from men, but that attention disappeared pretty quickly when they found out who she was and what she did for a living.

"Forget it." Gwen shrugged it off. "I didn't really mean it like that. I mean…"

"I keep forgetting what you do for a living," Deanna said. "I mean, it's crazy to me that you can do that for a *job*. Oh, but I didn't mean it like that. I'm sorry, Gwen. It's just—"

"It's fine. I totally get it. It is crazy. I'm not offended." She decided to change tact and confide in the one person who would totally understand. "But you know what *did* offend me?"

Her friend froze on the sidewalk and waited.

"Ian McCormick." She pronounced every syllable of his name with an edge.

"Ian? You saw him?"

"You know he's here?"

Deanna blinked at her mildly before she put a smile back on her face and ushered Gwen down the sidewalk. "You know what? Let's drop your bag off and then you can tell me all about it over a cup of coffee."

Gwen eyed her friend and shook her head. "How about a *drink*?"

"Why didn't you tell me Ian McCormick was here?" Gwen sat across from Deanna at her kitchen table, a glass of soda water in her hand. She'd gone for the soda, deciding against alcohol. It was her default drink, but now that she had it, she wished she'd gone for something stronger after all. *Ian McCormick was in Cedar Springs.* That had not been part of the plan. Not at all. Sure, whenever she thought of her summers in Cedar Springs visiting her grandma, Ian figured largely in her memory. Whether he knew it or not, his attention—or lack thereof, as was the case—had figured largely in her teenage life. She couldn't remember a summer she hadn't spent lusting after him. As one of the *summer* kids, he was kind of a celebrity among the local kids. Not that she'd been a local kid. But she also wasn't a summer kid. Gwen had definitely floated and never really had any friends except for Deanna.

Ian had no shortage of girls after him, but he'd never wanted to date any of them.

No. That wasn't true. He just hadn't wanted to date *her*. Not that she could blame him. If she'd been a teenage boy back then, *she* wouldn't have wanted to date her. Almost a hundred pounds overweight, with bad hair and glasses, she was a walking cliché. Hell, she was even more of a cliché now that she'd lost all the weight, turned her life around and was returning to her past childhood haunts. She was a made-for-TV movie, for goodness sake.

"I honestly didn't think it mattered." Deanna joined her at the table. "He's a summer kid."

"A...he's not a kid anymore. And, B...you know he's way more than that. He's *way more.*"

Deanna almost spat out her water. "No."

"No what?"

"No way you still have a thing for Ian McCormick."

Gwen didn't even have to answer that question, because the woman she'd always considered to be her best friend knew her well enough to know the answer. Or, she should have known her better than that, anyway. She narrowed her eyes and tilted her head.

"No way." Deanna shook her head. "Gwen, how can you possibly still be hung up on him? Honestly, I thought maybe after...well..."

"We said we'd never talk about that, remember?"

The situation they were never to discuss was a moment that could have broken up their friendship forever, but the girls made a decision not to let it affect them. Even though it had been hard, very hard for Gwen. The last summer she'd come to visit, Ian had arrived earlier than he usually had and somehow, Deanna and Ian ended up together at a party where they drank too much and...Gwen didn't like to think about it, but Deanna lost her virginity to Ian McCormick. She could have let it destroy their friendship, but Deanna felt terribly about it and she swore she'd never been more than just a friend with Ian and that's all it would ever be.

"Still," Deanna said. "I honestly didn't think you'd still be thinking of him at all."

How could she not? When they were kids, he'd actually been nice to her. He even talked to her and the conversations they had were real. Not about stupid stuff where she had to pretend to be interested in whatever football team was going to the playoffs or who got drunk at whatever party. But real stuff like what they hoped to achieve with their lives, what the future looked like and where they wanted to go to college. And besides that, he'd been so gorgeous. Correction, he *was* gorgeous. Maybe even more so, if that was possible.

But he still doesn't know you're alive, Gwen, the little voice in her head reminded her. She wasn't more than a townie friend back then, and she was even less now.

"So, he didn't recognize you?" Deanna changed tack. "Not that I'm surprised. You look like a totally different person. Seriously, if I didn't know better, I wouldn't even recognize you and we've been friends since…well, forever. You look crazy good."

Gwen blushed and waved away the compliment. She couldn't seem to get used to the attention she got from people who knew her *when.* It was almost easier for people to think she was just naturally thin and fit. Except when it came to her blog. But talking about her experiences online was a totally different thing. It was safe to hide behind the screen.

In fact, throughout her transformation, it had been a sort of therapy almost. Her website was the place she went to decompress and work through all the feelings that went along with her journey.

She should blog about Ian. Why hadn't she thought of that earlier? It made perfect sense. She could have a chance to process her feelings about seeing him again. *And still being invisible.* And she'd already made her summer vacation into an *event.* When she'd announced her plans to return to Cedar Springs, her readers had gone wild. They wrote in, offering suggestions as to how she should present her transformed self to her old friends, what she should do for a part-time job, and pretty much everything in between. It never ceased to amaze her how invested her readers were in her life and her weight loss journey. In fact, the whole *returning home* thing had garnered so much attention that a talent agent, Jade Johnson, had contacted Gwen about representation, a book deal, and a possible television deal. It was all too crazy to comprehend, but Gwen wasn't about to say no.

She swallowed the rest of her water quickly. "The next one needs alcohol."

"Really?"

Gwen nodded. "Yes. There are only sixty-four calories in vodka. And I'll just run a few extra miles tomorrow. It'll be worth it."

Deanna laughed. "Sounds good. Well, not the running part. I'll leave that up to you. But I don't have any patients tomorrow, so I'll have a few drinks to toast your return. I'll get Marcus to meet us at the Grizzly Paw when he's done up at the hill. He'll want to meet you. I have trouble remembering that you never knew him."

"Nope." Gwen shook her head. "He moved here after my last summer. But it sounds like a good plan to me." Gwen leaned down to retrieve her laptop from the bag at her feet. "But first I need to post an entry."

"Seriously? You just got here."

"I know." She smiled and tried not to take offense to her friend's expression. Ever since her blog started to get real attention and had actually started to make her money, most people had the same reaction. She'd definitely discovered that people struggled with the idea that you could actually make a living writing about your life. Hell, when the advertising offers had first started coming in, Gwen had trouble believing anyone would actually want to give her money to tell her story. "But it pays the bills, Dee. So as long as people want to read it, I'm going to write it."

She flipped open her laptop, signed onto Deanna's Wi-Fi and logged into her account before her fingers froze over the keys. "What do you think?" she asked her friend. "How should I write about Ian?"

"Ian?" Deanna shook her head. "You can't. I mean, you can't use his name or anything."

"Oh my God. Of course not! I don't use anyone's real name. I don't even say what town I'm in. That part is all anonymous. It has to be. But part of the success of everything is how real it all is. So…"

"You're going to blog about Ian?"

Gwen nodded. There really wasn't a question about it. In fact, she'd already kind of alluded to him in past posts as one of her catalysts for starting her weight loss journey. There was no doubt in her mind that if she'd been thin all those years ago, Ian would never have stood her up at the Summer Equinox festival. Not a chance.

"Wait." Deanna got that look in her eye that meant she'd just figured out the connection. "You've already blogged about him, haven't you?"

"You read my blog?"

Deanna gave her a look. "Of course I do. Since the beginning. And that's when you mentioned…Ian is Mr. Summer. How did I not see that until right now?"

Gwen laughed. "I have no idea. It's not like my feelings for him were a big secret or anything. Doesn't everyone remember my public humiliation?"

Deanna grabbed her hand and squeezed. "Gwen, no one remembers that. I promise."

"I remember."

Her friend laughed a little and moved away. "You're the only one. It wasn't even a big deal. He just didn't show up. It's not important. Let it go."

But as Deanna moved about the kitchen, cleaning up dishes and leaving Gwen to write her blog post, all she could think of was that it *was* important and there was no way she could let it go.

Dear Reader,

Sometimes things don't turn out quite the way you plan...

If you're anything like me, you've spent some time thinking about and maybe even daydreaming about how certain people from your past will react to seeing the new and healthier version of you after wronging you. Not to say that I've spent a lot of time thinking on this, but I'd be lying if I said I never thought of it. Of course, as I was planning my return to the town I'd spent all my summers, there was one person in particular that came to mind. Mr. Summer. Long-time readers will remember me mentioning Mr. Summer before. Every young woman—particularly those of us who've struggled with our body image...who hasn't—has at least one encounter with a boy or man that has stuck with them. An encounter for better or worse that somehow shaped or defined how they thought of members of the opposite sex, and sadly, how they thought of themselves.

That was Mr. Summer. I was desperately in love with him from the summers of fourteen to eighteen. Four years of my life in which he barely knew I was alive. When he finally did notice me, he humiliated me and broke my heart.

For years, he was the star of my fantasies when I thought about returning with my new and improved self. How would he react? Would his jaw drop? Would he stumble over his words as he apologized for standing me up all those years ago? Would he beg me to give him another chance?

Well, readers, I can tell you that now, all these years later I finally have my answer.

None of those things happened. In fact, he didn't even recognize me.

We came eye to eye and there wasn't even a flicker of acknowledgment in his eyes. (Which are still as dreamy as I remember.)

And now I'm here, on the eve of my first night back in town and already I'm filled with a strong sense of dissatisfaction in regards to Mr. Summer. So, obviously I cannot let a homecoming come and go without doing something about it. Or can I?

What do you think? Should I confront Mr. Summer and thank him for being at least one of the catalysts that spurred my life change? Or should I let it go and move on? Or maybe something different….

Will Gwen let Ian know that they've met? Or will she play a game with him? And if she does…who will win?
Find out NOW! Read Love in the Moment for FREE!

About the Author

Elena Aitken is a USA Today Bestselling Author of more than forty romance and women's fiction novels. Living a stone's throw from the Rocky Mountains with her teenager twins, their two cats and a goofy rescue dog, Elena escapes into the mountains whenever life allows. She can often be found with her toes in the lake and a glass of wine in her hand, dreaming up her next book and working on her own happily ever after with her very own mountain man.

To learn more about Elena:
www.elenaaitken.com
elena@elenaaitken.com